TILL A BETTER WORLD:

A Novel

NADIJA MUJAGIC

UNITED STATES OF AMERICA

EMMA'S LIFE WAS GOING TO CHANGE, FOR BETTER OR for worse, in a matter of hours. The CEO called her into his office a couple of hours earlier. She had no clue what to expect. She was nervous, as she considered the possibility she might have done something to rattle his cage, but she couldn't quite think of any recent incidents. He rarely called her to his office. *Something must be up.*

As she approached his office, she felt uneasy. If he had anything negative to say, she already decided she'd listen to him carefully, ask any questions, and decide later what to do. But with her work ethic, Emma would have been shocked to hear anything even slightly undesirable or negative.

When she opened the door, he was sitting behind his desk, smiling. Derek's youthful looks belied his age. It was quite possible he was dyeing his hair, but even so, with his tall stature and muscular body, he did not resemble a man in his sixties. He had been with the company for a couple of decades already and he had reached the executive level long ago. As the CEO, he was powerful and he exuded confidence. His peers had high regard and respect for him and when Derek was highly enthusiastic about an idea, they'd be careful to disagree with him. None of his ideas failed. That's why he seemed invincible.

Derek smiled at Emma as she gingerly opened the door. She peeked her head first, before stepping in. She was dressed in a navy-blue suit by Calvin Klein, her favorite brand. She had a slim body, but it wasn't because she was diligent in running on the treadmill every morning. It was because stress would eat away at her, as she worried about every single little thing. Even when things in her life were going splendidly, she'd find a reason to panic. She'd have nightmares frequently, as if she purposefully carried her worries into her dreams. But she couldn't help it. Her tendency to worry, she suspected, was the reason she had been highly successful in her life goals. Emma knew that if she ever let her hair down, things would be different. She'd somehow fail.

When she stood in his office, she wondered if she had somehow failed him. But his wide smile put her at ease.

"Well, Emma. Thank you for coming to see me. Please sit." He extended his arm and pointed to the leather chair on the other side of his desk. "I have read reports about your performance the last year, and I have heard a lot of good things about you from your peers and executives alike. Your customers are happy, your stats are incredible. In this tough market, we can't afford to lose you—not that you're looking for another job. The executive team and the board of directors have decided to offer you a promotion."

Emma's eyes widened. She had not expected this. For her, her work ethic was simply the norm, not something she should be rewarded for.

"That is extremely generous. I'm not sure what to say."

"The new position we'd like to offer you is an Executive Director for the Northeastern region. If you accept, you'll be leading a team of seven professionals."

"That's an incredible opportunity, Mr. Shultz." Her feet were tapping restlessly against the floor; she could feel her palms sweating and her heartbeat had quickened. She had never been offered a promotion before, and she had certainly never asked for one. Her modesty never let her demand anything of anyone or ask for special treatment.

"Oh, call me Derek." He smiled. "Feel free to think about it. But let me know as soon as possible since there's a lot of work to be done, and soon."

"I'll take it." She responded as fast as she could. Those student loans wouldn't pay themselves.

"Excellent. Excellent," Derek said, never losing his smile. "I'm planning on announcing your promotion to the whole company on Monday, and your new title will be in effect two weeks from now."

"Thank you, Derek. I am grateful for this

opportunity."

"You're quite welcome." He stood up and extended his arm to shake her hand. "We are so happy to have you here. You deserve this promotion. I hope you'll be pleased to hear that it also comes with a higher salary. You're getting a twenty percent increase."

"That's fantastic." She smiled.

She returned to her office and sat down on her chair, looking at the plant in a corner of the room. It looked bright and lovely, and she was surprised to see it. She had not noticed it before. Out of excitement, she didn't know what to do next—try to focus on her work or call her family and husband to break the news—so she decided for something completely different. She went downstairs to the cafeteria to get herself a cup of coffee. Out the window, she saw the blue sky decorated by a couple of clouds—the spring in Boston was beckoning, melting the snow and making puddles and rivers that dissipated into the ground.

She hurried home to break the news. She found Michael sitting at his computer when she arrived.

"Hey, honey. How are you?" She came up to him and kissed the top of his head.

"Fine," Michael said.

"How's your job search?" When Michael graduated from business school, Emma had high hopes he'd land a lucrative job that would pay him six figures right off the bat to help them pay off their student loans. Before moving to Boston, he'd worked as a bartender in his home town in Minnesota. He'd get tired of the late-night shifts, the dicks and bimbos waving at him for his attention and people leaving meager tips. He'd resolved to make a sudden shift in his career and, having a knack for numbers and people (or so he thought), he took a GMAT, scored nearly perfectly and applied to the best business schools in the country. He was astonished to learn that all five wanted him. He chose the one in Cambridge, Massachusetts because, of the five letters, it was the first one he received.

"I have a couple of interviews on Monday." He smiled. Michael was covered in tattoos, remnants of his bartending days—and for this reason Emma didn't think that people took him seriously. This was his tenth interview in a month. Nothing had materialized so far. Whenever she asked him if he'd consider removing the one that well reached the tip of his fingers and his neck, a griffin, he'd stubbornly say that he could do his job with or without the tattoos.

"That's fantastic, honey." She couldn't wait to break the news. Part of her still felt like it was all a dream. "I'm getting a big promotion at work." She couldn't stop smiling.

"What? You've been waiting all day to tell me?"

"I wanted to tell you in person. It's a big deal. I'm getting a twenty percent raise."

"Wow. They're not kidding around. Congrats, baby."

"I bought a bottle of wine so we can celebrate

tonight." Now that her promotion was set in stone, she held high hopes for their future. They came closer to buying a house and growing a family.

Coincidentally, a week after her promotion announcement, Michael ended up getting an entry-level manager job in a tech company in Kendall Square. His salary was in the low eighties, which was okay for Boston, but not high enough to quickly pay off their student loans, which had amounted to three times his starting salary. But Emma wanted to be supportive of Michael no matter what.

When the much-anticipated day of her promotion finally arrived, Emma woke up early in the morning and started getting ready for work in her one-bedroom Cambridge apartment.

One of the few apartments she and Michael, could afford in Cambridge was this one, located between First and Third Streets, overlooking the tallest building on their block: a cement edifice that wouldn't be considered so unattractive were it not indeed a jail, not the first sight Emma wanted to have every morning.

When she and Michael had first moved in, the kitchen faucet was wobbly and water dripped rom it with vengeance. The landlord hadn't responded to their request to replace it until they threatened to give notice and move out. Luckily he had, because otherwise, where else would they go? It wasn't as if they were swimming in an ocean of choices; that was reserved for the wealthy. They'd scrambled to get used furniture on Craigslist, trying to cut the corners and save money whenever they could. The only good news was that her current work-place was within reasonable walking distance.

On the official day of her promotion, her morning ritual began earlier than usual. She first made coffee in the kitchen, then worked out on a treadmill in a corner of her bedroom, and then took a long shower, indulging in the extra steps of using a fancy body scrub and a hair mask to allow herself a moment before the long day. After the shower, she carefully picked from the selection of clothes lined up in her crowded and tiny walk-in closet, picking jewelry that matched her new suit.

Now that the spring arrived and much of the snow on the sidewalks was gone, she decided she would walk to her office, a twenty-minute distance from her house. Before she exited the apartment, she checked herself in the hallway mirror one more time to fix any makeup imperfections. The morning was cloudy and damp, so wearing rubber rain boots became her obvious choice. She would change into stilettos when she arrived in the office.

The block Emma lived on was infamous for its narrow sidewalks, with its cracked pavement and uneven ground. Trees protruded through the asphalt and the growing and stretching roots would wreak havoc on the paths. She walked on the sidewalks by lifting her feet up high to ensure she wouldn't trip or fall. She cracked a smile when she pictured a spectator watching the funny image of her lifting her feet up high in her rubber boots.

On her leisurely walk to the office, she hoped she'd clear her head and find her happy space before the day turned chaotic. The streets were quiet; only a car or two would pass by her. She saw a young man running for the bus, the one that she often took to work. The man looked slim and he ran fast. The bus pulled over at the bus stop, and the young man stormed onto the bus. Emma nodded and smiled when she saw he made it.

She walked by two-family and single houses and couldn't help but whisper to herself, "My goodness, they're so close to each other." Some houses were painted bright colors, while others were in a state of disrepair. She wondered if the old houses might have been inherited by families who couldn't otherwise afford to live in and care for the house. The Boston area was expensive.

It was the year 2008, and the real estate market bubble was about to burst, bringing Emma hope that she and Michael could snatch up an affordable home. Even with her promotion, one thing that stood in the path of that dream was their exorbitant student loans. Emma was appalled to learn that even if she declared bankruptcy, the ugly student loans would still hang over her broke-ass head until they were paid off. Instead of her mother reading her books when she was a small child, maybe she should have taught her to bake. At least then, she might have a lucrative bakery right now, and the peace of mind that comes with it. But, sometimes, fate is not to be argued with, because—what was the point?

She passed by the row of houses and found herself on vibrant Mass Ave, bustling with people and traffic. Every time Emma walked on this familiar path, she noticed stores she hadn't noticed before. It was quite possible that some of them were recently opened; though, she ultimately reasoned that she hadn't notice them because she focused too much on anticipating seeing the restaurant where Michael proposed to her a couple of years back. After all, the restaurant brought out a happy memory, and she latched onto it more than to noticing a random store.

The restaurant reminded her of the happy days when she first started dating Michael. Ever since they met in business school, Emma had felt safer, more protected, having him around. When they prepared for exams, they studied together, sharing notes on case studies and essays. He'd offered all his thoughts and insights in a way that resembled him telling her his deepest secrets. Whenever she spoke, he'd listen to her intently, staring into her brown eyes.

Michael didn't seem to be her type physically—way too low a BMI on his six-foot, two-inch body, an occasional pimple on his face and eyeglasses one might deem too thick. But his other qualities were all she wanted in a man. Hard working, intelligent, thoughtful, kind... He constantly made her laugh. When they took breaks from studying, she would inquire about his family, often wondering how he ended up in the business school.

After their first date, which had lasted until nearly two in the morning, Emma and Michael spent more time together, not as classmates, but as a promising new couple. When that school year finished, and they both graduated, feeling that sense they were on their way to better and bigger things, Michael proposed to her in that same restaurant on Mass Ave. He had asked the hostess to put the diamond ring in her ice cream dessert.

When Emma noticed the diamond protruding from her bowl, she yelped and brought her hands to her mouth in surprise.

"Oh my god, oh my god. Yes. Yes, I do!" she exclaimed as loud claps filled the room. Without even realizing it, she added, "I can't wait to have children with you."

That night, as they waltzed to the music in their apartment, half-drunk, Emma reached for Michael's neck to hug him, dreaming about what their children might look like.

Emma's thoughts were disrupted when she noticed a heavyset woman looking distraught, walking from the opposite direction with a child hand in hand. The girl might have been three or four; her steps seemed unstable and weak. The girl wore a yellow raincoat and black tights, tiny sneakers on her feet. The girl's body bounced as she tried to keep up with the woman's pace. She had no expression on her face. Her long blonde hair danced like waves, and the woman suddenly pulled her, telling her to hurry even though the girl was already making effort to do so.

I wish I could give this little girl a hug, Emma thought. She looked at her, hoping their eyes would lock as they passed, but the girl's eyes remained focused ahead. At every sight of a child, Emma's heart grew tender. But today, she tried to dismiss that feeling, as she had a more important task at hand.

Arriving at work on the first day she'd have her new job title of Executive Director, she felt all eyes on her—the eyes of her coworkers. She could tell they were wondering what special skills she possessed to have been promoted. For as long as Emma worked for corporate giants, she had known that whenever a woman got a job promotion, it was questioned. When a man got a promotion, it was expected, no big deal.

Emma didn't care about those looks and continued walking toward her new office, which was situated in a corner of the building, two doors down from Derek's. When she entered the office, the CONGRATULATIONS banner placed on the wall immediately caught her eye. She touched it gently, as if it were the Holy Grail. She sat at her desk and stared at her computer, trying to feel the joy and success surrounding her. Even though she now felt accomplished professionally, she still felt an emptiness; something was missing, something in her heart she wanted more keenly. As she was daydreaming, a knock on her door startled her.

"Good morning, Emma. How are you?" A short, middle-aged woman with perm-curly hair and eyeglasses appeared at her office door.

"I'm good." Emma had to pause for a second. She didn't recognize the woman at all. "Can I help you?"

"Oh, I just wanted to say hi. I'm Mary. Derek said I'm going to be your assistant. You will share my time with another executive director, but not to worry—I'm quite good at time management and I'm super organized." She smiled.

"Excellent. Thank you, Mary," said Emma. "If you don't mind me asking, how long have you been with the company? I'm ashamed to say I don't remember seeing you here before."

Mary laughed. "Oh, no worries. I move so fast that I've become a blur in the office." She laughed again. "About six years."

Emma couldn't help her reaction. She exclaimed, "Wow, that's a long time. Have you always worked in this department?"

"Yes, I have. As a matter of fact, I've been in the same position since I arrived at the company. You know, I don't really care about promotions and all that career development stuff." She then lowered her voice and continued. "I'm a single mother." Her head nodded in approval to indicate that this was the most important thing Emma should know about her.

"I have three children, and I raised them all alone. One is still a teenager, while the other two are in college. I needed a safe job and benefits, and I have both here." She looked around the office to reaffirm what she meant by here.

"That's incredible, Mary." Emma reached for a pen on her desk and began to twirl it in her hand. She stared at Mary, studying her with an empty look on her face. Emma thought that Mary seemed too chubby and short; her hair looked old-fashioned; her slacks wedged deep in her rear and her blouse with flower prints looked too short—and what was with her eyeglasses? But she was a mother. Of three, no less.

To break the awkward silence, Mary continued, "And so you know, I'll be connecting my calendar to yours so I know your availability for meetings."

"That's great. I appreciate it. I'll be doing my best to do my own scheduling, though. Otherwise, I'd forget all my meetings." She didn't want Mary, or anyone else, to run her life. She was in full control.

"That's no problem. Whatever, whenever you need anything, let me know. I'm around." Mary turned around and disappeared from Emma's sight.

Emma relaxed in her chair, closed her eyes and breathed in and out slowly, sucking in all the good vibes she was feeling. She patted down her long red hair and quickly pulled a mirror out of her purse to check her makeup.

As she looked at her face, she noticed her expression slowly turn into a grimace. Emma's life would be happier and more successful if it were completed by having children of her own. She couldn't quite pinpoint where her strong desire to have a baby came from—her family wasn't a good role model and she was certain it didn't come from her childhood—but it was something that consumed her every waking thought.

She'd grown up in a suburb of Chicago with a mother who was a pre-school teacher, and a father who was a not-so-successful car salesman. Their house was tiny, two bedrooms, one bath, and its slight stature stood out against the mini-mansions of the neighborhood. When

Emma's little sister Belinda was born, her parents talked about buying a newer, roomier home, but ultimately could only daydream. They couldn't even always pay their bills on time. Her father, Russell, wasn't the best salesman and his commissions often fell under expectations. While her mother's monthly income was steady, it was still a teacher's salary, just above minimum wage.

While his youth still bloomed, her father lost his purpose in life. His parents weren't there when he needed love the most. Emma's grandfather often called him strange depreciating names, like Milkman or Mr. Goofy, and those images distorted his self-worth. The nicknames didn't match his looks, though, since he was a good-looking boy, with a cheek dimple, deep blue eyes, and luscious hair. Her father never really understood why he was given those names. Girls eyed him, but he would only duck his head, wanting to hide, and when he was a teenager, he found his love of the drink. He had his first beer with his neighbor Perry, a boy a few years older than he, a loner whom he saw as a kindred spirit. From there on, her father drank often and much; maybe he should have been a fish.

As a grown, married man, her father would frequent a bar a couple of blocks from the dealership. He'd order one, two, three shots until he'd lose a sense of time. And then he'd order a couple more until he could barely walk. He'd come home, zig-zagging the streets of Chicago, and crash on the couch. Emma had gotten used to him being this way. He wasn't violent. He never raised his hand on his children. And even though he was a heavy drinker, he'd still get up in the morning and go to work.

It took years for her to realize that her dad was depressed, lacking self-esteem. She knew he felt like he could have done much more for his family, but he just kept on failing. His life would have been better off had he chosen to visit a therapist and sort his anxieties out, but he was a baby boomer, and didn't see the value in it as it would be an admission of failure. He just soaked in the feeling of hard work and success of his generational peers.

When Emma moved to Cambridge, she often feared the dreadful phone call informing her that her father had been found in a ditch somewhere, in his infamous blue suit, the smell of alcohol emanating from his body. Ultimately, she didn't see her father as much of a parental figure, but more like a live rubber doll disheveled and lost in time and space.

Emma's mother, Bella, never showed disgust or disappointment towards her husband. She'd held so much empathy for him that at night, she'd cry for him. When her mother was younger, she'd frequently visit the local church and Emma recalled some of the prayers her mother would repeat as her father lay on the couch looking lifeless.

Almighty God, we entrust all who are dear to us to thy never-failing care and love, for this life and the life to come, knowing that thou art doing for them better things than we can desire or pray for; through Jesus Christ our Lord. Amen.

But the prayers didn't bear fruit. Her father remained his old diffident self.

Regardless of her upbringing, Emma's desire to have children was a simple fact, a part of her being, equaled to her desk being made of wood or the ocean being blue. She had no other explanation for it.

There was something about having children that Emma thought was sacred. The instant they are conceived, the mother feels an indescribable connection to the new human inside her. The baby grows like a seed for which a woman serves as earth, water, and sun. When baby's heart comes alive, those beats pump love through woman's veins to her brain. And when the baby is born, the mother's love is undeniable. Unconditional. It is rooted in her being forever.

Emma and Michael had been trying to conceive, but to no avail.

A few days after she started her new job, she visited her physician for a routine appointment. She had scheduled this appointment several months in advance. During her visit, the doctor took her blood, urine, checked her blood pressure, and did a pap smear.

On her way home, tired from the ordeal, she stopped by a local bakery and grabbed a couple of her favorite delicacies, hoping that they would make her feel better. She came home and curled up in bed by seven p.m., fast asleep, and did not wake up until dawn.

Her test results came out a few days after her appointment.

"Your tests results are all normal." Her physician

announced over the phone. Emma took that as good news, but they puzzled her at the same time.

"So, why we have not seen any results, doctor?"

"I can't tell why," the doctor said. "I suggest you see a gynecologist, who can work with you closely and tell you about your options."

A few weeks later, on her doctor's suggestion, she went to an OB/GYN. Filled with hope all over again, she told the OB that *she must have kids or else...* Or else? Emma didn't know how to end this thought. If she didn't have kids, she'd be lost. Her world would remain empty.

"Emma, as far as I can tell, there's nothing wrong with your body," the gynecologist said over the phone. "Your blood test didn't show any abnormalities. The ultrasound turned out normal, as well. Your egg count is where it should be for your age, which means you still have plenty time left to have children."

"That's good news, doctor." She paused. "So, why haven't I been able to get pregnant?" She clenched her fist and closed her eyes, as if to prepare herself for the worst possible answer.

"It doesn't mean you *can't* get pregnant. It just means that you need to keep trying. If you're not successful within the next three months, call me and we can plan the next steps. Does that sound good?"

She wasn't sure if that sounded good. In fact, she thought three months was way too long. She felt mortified that another potential failure could be ahead of her.

"Stay away from stress and don't think too much

about all this," the OB continued. "If you relax and enjoy the process, you'll increase your chance of conceiving."

They hung up and Emma began to cry uncontrollably. Three months. The world could flip upside down in months. In August, she was turning thirty-eight and her biological clock was screaming at her. She stormed into the bedroom to hide her tears from Michael, crawled into her bed, and whispered prayers.

2

BOSNIA AND HERZEGOVINA

SHORTLY AFTER THE BOSNIAN WAR ENDED, PEOPLE scrambled to find any type of work to sustain their wellbeing. Selma lucked out when she had walked by KONZUM, the only supermarket in the airport neighborhood. It was the year 2008, and the country hadn't seen much economic improvement since peace arrived at the end of the war. Hope was a hot commodity. She had eyed the sign on the door saying they were hiring. When she entered the store, she found herself standing at the cash register, with the narrow paths between the aisles on the side. She liked the size of the place—not too big to get lost, but not too small either to feel claustrophobic.

A middle-aged woman greeted her. She looked cranky, or bored, or both. The bags under her eyes were hanging like two big punching bags, her rose lipstick covered her thin lips, and her curly hair was disheveled, revealing a couple inches of gray roots. Her turtleneck covered her double chin and the wrinkles on her face had accumulated over the years. She certainly looked like she was trying too hard to look decent for the customers.

It was no secret the war had wiped off smiles from people's faces. Including Selma's. Yet she stood in front of the woman, waiting for her to say something, perhaps offer a smile to make her feel at ease. But the woman kept her stern look, growing more annoyed as she made a face.

"Can I help you?"

"I'd like to apply for the open job."

The woman didn't say anything but bent over to grab something—a piece of paper that turned out to be the job application.

"Here. Fill this out and give it back to me."

Selma grabbed it from her. This piece of paper would determine her near future. She needed to find a job to prove she was capable of taking care of herself.

She began to fill it out on the spot.

Name: Selma Karic
Date of birth: April 2, 1982
Place of birth: Doboj, Bosnia
Prior work experience:

She paused. She virtually had no work experience. But if she were to make something up, maybe it would get her the job.

Prior work experience: waitress.
Earliest day available to work: Immediately.

She handed the application back to the woman, looking her straight in the eye as if that might charm her into helping her get it. The woman looked down at the application, and without raising her head, said, "I'll give this to the manager. She will call you."

The following day, Selma's phone rang, a rare occurrence. On the other line was the supermarket manager informing her she got the job. She told her to be on the premises the following day at seven in the morning. Selma obeyed the command, and bright and early the next day, heavy-eyed, she showed up eager to help them carry the merchandise from the storage room to the shelves.

Every day after work seemed pretty much the same. She'd stop by her favorite bakery on the corner of her street, grab a couple of pastries for dinner—and breakfast the following day—and head home. She always hurried, her legs shuffling on the street as if someone was chasing her.

Stray dogs, always in a pack of six or seven, lingered on the streets, skinny and disheveled, and they'd constantly be looking for food, lurking behind corners, hoping for a bite or two. People complained about the dogs all the time, especially those with young children, and hoped the city would do something about them, perhaps by building a shelter to house and domesticate them until they found new owners. Like most people in

the post-war country, the dogs, too, felt lost and directionless without a stable home to return to. Rumors said
they attacked people at night. But not Selma. While the
neighbors watched her inquisitively, the dogs, for some
reason, left her alone, perhaps realizing she, too, had it
hard.

As long as she was employed, her days and mind
eased. The work distracted her from the turmoil in her
head. When the supermarket wasn't busy with
customers, she would find something to do, like replace
the inventory, count the merchandise, put price labels on
items, and shelve them. At eight p.m. sharp every day, the
doors of the supermarket closed, ending Selma's work
shift.

Before Selma clocked out from her night shift one
cold January evening, she went behind the deli counter to
grab her purse. She opened the box of pills she always
carried and put one in her mouth, swallowing it with a
sip of her bottled water, almost instantly feeling relief.

How much longer do I need to keep taking these?

Ever since she began taking them, her anxiety had
been largely at bay. The panic attacks she used to get had
dwindled over time, but she still felt their remainders
underneath her skin, itching to come out and make her
life difficult. Like being locked in a coffin, she felt she
had no place to go.

Sarajevo wasn't quite the city she dreamed of living in.
Still recovering from the war, the city's landscape looked
like some drunk buffoon just threw all his trash into a
neighbor's backyard. Mosques were finally beginning to

rise again from the landscape like wild mushrooms. They were built in awkward locations between buildings, next to playgrounds, near daycares and schools, and their minarets were stretching to the sky.

Before the war, the city felt rather claustrophobic surrounded by the tall deep green mountains and enveloped by smog. Yet, people rarely ventured out. Occasionally, they'd make a trip to the mountains and watch the smog form at the edges of the landscape. In the summer, they'd travel to Croatia to enjoy the smell of the iridescent Adriatic Sea and the vastness of star shine shimmering in the water. When the war began, one thing was certain: the majority of people didn't think it would come to their city. And now, like in the pre-war days, people chose not to go anywhere. It was as if the idea of escaping the war was like attending a picnic in a mountain park—delightful but voluntary.

In the dreadful days of early April 1992, Sarajevo fell into arms of the enemy. Serbs positioned themselves on top of the hills and mountains, where just a few months earlier, people had enjoyed hiking and downhill skiing. In a matter of days, the city was transformed into a space that might have resembled a locked psych ward room where mad men were randomly shooting at its bare walls with guns and tanks. Eventually, Sarajevo looked like an old, rusty car, damaged and malfunctioning, abandoned in a junk yard: some buildings collapsed, almost all were splattered by bullets, shells, and shrapnel, a number of bridges over the Miljacka River destroyed. The National Library burned to ashes along with the history and scripts it housed; the city parks were stripped of trees, their branches used to start fires in cold powerless homes; even the sky looked pierced with gloom and pain.

The city stayed under siege for three and a half years, the longest in modern history. Local street thugs took advantage of the chaos and anarchy, some amplifying their thuggy-ness with guns while others became outright war criminals, stealing, raping and killing.

Selma didn't find comfort in this city. The place didn't belong to her, and she didn't belong to it. But she had no choice in the matter. Her own past constantly lingered in her mind, breathing heaviness upon her psyche. Her memories were selective, often going back to her childhood when her parents were still around, when all she cared about was playing games and spending time with friends or watching cartoons. If she had had a choice, she would not have chosen this life. If God did exist, and he was the one who dealt cards, he was a cruel wretch, a bastard she would punch in the invisible face if she could.

Against the surrounding mountains, Igman and Trebevic, the streets seemed darker, more dangerous. But Selma didn't care, because her new apartment was a couple of blocks away, a fifteen-minute walk. Along the street stood vendors with carts selling boiled corn and chestnuts, enticing passerby with their comforting smell. The vendors brought their hands to their mouths to warm themselves up. Good jobs were hard to find in the post-war city and while the sellers had hoped the business would be as lucrative as before the war, only a few customers took the bait.

Whenever she walked down the street, the people would look at her and say under their breath: this poor thing. But Selma wanted not to think of herself as either poor or a thing; in search of herself, she wasn't quite sure what exactly she was. Poor, maybe. A thing, also a slight possibility. If she were to suppress her past and feelings, she could easily turn her into a *thing*.

It seemed that the world consisted of the space contained in Selma's shadow; and sometimes memories. Memories of the good past. She was happiest in the surroundings she had created herself: her modest apartment. The only safe space.

Memories flooded her unexpectedly, trying to reconcile her past. She often unearthed good memories, not on her own volition, in order to sustain her livelihood. People who occupied her childhood the most came to visit her mind, like a gentle knock on the door.

She'd think of Mirza, her neighbor she had grown up with. They were the same age, living in close proximity in Kotorsko, a village close to Doboj city. As kids, they'd chase butterflies in the nearby field and walk in the stream with the freezing water at their feet. Their parents both had chickens in a small fenced part of the yard, and her favorite part of her day was walking around looking for eggs. She'd find them in the dog house, in the grass near the water well, in the chicken coop. Her mother, Aisha, would give her a bowl to collect them in and she would then store her finds, or prepare them to sell at the farmer's market. As well as the eggs, her family grew and sold vegetables and fruits. The business was not lucrative—her parents never expected to get rich off it—but it provided basic necessities for their family of four.

The village she had lived in was decorated with small hills and streams where the community spent their time, lounging on the grass or soaking feet in the cold water. Hobbies were a notion for the educated and rich. Selma had never played sport, or picked up a musical instrument.

A boy named Dragan who lived two houses down and was a couple of years older than Selma would take over whatever simple game the younger kids were playing and the dynamic would instantly change. The kids would pass the ball silently without any rowdiness or laughter and exchange looks between them, avoiding his gaze. Everyone knew, even the adults, that Dragan seemed a bit off—he was hyperactive, wild in nature—and some kids feared his lack of fear for everything and everyone that crossed his path.

Once, he saw Selma walking through the field on her way home from school and crossed her path with his arms reaching out as if he was about to give her a hug. He had skipped the school that day—again—and his parents set him free to roam around the village, hoping he'd find a good distraction or that someone would take pity on the young boy and spend quality time with him. But all heads turned the opposite way whenever they saw Dragan and his evil little look.

Selma was startled by Dragan's appearance from the middle of nowhere. She felt like she were Little Red

Riding Hood being approached by the wolf. Her home stood nearby, yet it seemed so far.

"Where are you heading?" Dragan yelled.

"Home," she said, trying not to show her fear.

"I'm not gonna let you pass."

As much as Selma wanted to find an escape route, she stood there motionless. She waited for Dragan's next move.

When the boy noticed that Selma was not reacting, he said, "You can go if you lick the butterfly powder from my finger."

He extended his pointer finger toward her.

"I'm not licking your finger."

"You are if you wanna go home today." An evil smile formed on his face.

"No!"

"Well, then, we can stand here all day and all night if need be." He crossed his arms and watched her with suspicion.

"Let me see your finger." Her curiosity had taken away her fear. She wanted to know what this butterfly wing dust looked like. She didn't know what it was, though, many a time she'd go on the field, catch butterflies of all colors and place them in a jar. She was fascinated by them and would watch as they flew in the small space until they gave up and slowly landed on the jar bottom, lifeless.

Dragan took a step closer and extended his finger. The dust looked yellow and dense, soft even, like an unidentified powder one might encounter in a makeup case. It looked perfectly ordinary, yet Selma found it simple and beautiful at the same time. Selma grabbed his finger and quickly licked it, leaving his skin clean.

Surprised by her resolve to do the unthinkable, he looked at her with his mouth agape, while she moved forward, brushing up against his shoulder, and marched ahead. She left him there, looking after her as if he'd just seen a ghost. Dragan, the kid with the reputation of being mean and harsh, had no idea that by catching the butterfly and stripping of its dust, he had shortened its lifespan, as short as it already was. Selma knew this about these beautiful creatures, and she also knew that if Dragan found out the same, he would most likely not care in the slightest.

In Kotorsko, things like this seemed nothing out of the ordinary. People acted on an impulse, but they easily forgot these mishaps and strange interactions. They were accepted as the norm, as something that happened in a place where no hobbies were had or no education cultivated.

When she arrived home, she decided to carry on as if nothing had happened.

Her parents' home was the pillar of their pride. Her father, Adem, had built this two-story sanctuary, brick by brick, before Selma was born when he beamed with health and strength. With his dark hair and skin, he looked different from the towering Bosnian men who had light complexions and blue eyes. Indeed, he was quite the opposite from them. Stocky and shorter than the average Bosnian man, her father had earnt the nickname *Crni* from his close friends—meaning black in Bosnian. His appearance wouldn't seem too startling if he were never in presence of his wife, Aisha, who was nearly a foot taller than him. In this country, people preferred to be paired with a partner of a suitable height, but living in Kotorsko didn't present too many options as far as meeting a variety people. It was like trying to marry within your own tribe, within the same physical and cultural boundaries. Her mother didn't mind that her husband was shorter than her, even though the village kids often made fun of them saying how his head could serve as a table for her to eat. On a bad day, Selma's father would cuss the children out and tell them to mind their own business, but Aisha would hold his hand and tell him to calm down; "Leave the kids alone, you can't reason with them."

Kotorsko was a place where no stray cats or dogs existed. Sure, the animals did exist, but they belonged to no one and everyone. Villagers' hospitality manifested itself through their allowing the animals to come in to their houses and go as they pleased. The animals were neither wild nor domestic. But they were tamed enough that they didn't bite.

Selma had a daily visitor, an orange cat they named Ginger after a character in *The Terminator*. In the movie, the cat had purposely been named a non-Yugoslav name in order to bring in a Western spice into their life. They worked on the pronunciation for days, *džin-džer, džin-džer*, until it got engrained into their minds. They had no idea that ginger was the word for the pungent root meant *djumbir* in their language. None of them spoke English.

Selma spent time with Ginger when Mirza wasn't around. In Kotorsko, you were bound to never feel alone or lonely.

Mirza had a similar upbringing to Selma, with his parents growing corn and selling it wholesale. His father often traveled around the country—which was named Yugoslavia back then—to procure contracts for the sale of his corn. Having only graduated from primary school, his education was limited, and his signature on the contracts looked a bit wobbly, as if a little kid who was just starting to learn to write had scribbled it. Mirza's mother had no education at all. Her signature would have been the single X the illiterate were told to place on a signature line.

Like Mirza's parents, Selma's too matched their education level. From generation to generation, they'd live in a farm and raise animals or grow produce and live peaceful lives with their like-minded neighbors.

Selma's and Mirza's mothers became closer as they saw their children playing together quietly, rarely causing trouble. The women would get together and have coffee practically every day to share their daily news about their farms. On occasion, they'd also share recipes for different types of jams they could make out of the fruits growing in their back yards.

"I have plenty of jars left if you need them," one would say.

"I'll take four or five so I don't need to go into town."

Selma and Mirza knew they were following their parents' path: despite projecting curiosity and desire to learn, they were destined to end up with the same limited education and become peasants. At times, Selma and Mirza would try to guess what life would be like outside their confined little world. Did Sarajevo, the Bosnian capital, have any tall buildings like the ones in New York City? Whenever their parents would watch the news from around the country on their black and white TV, they'd see glimpses of the city. The letters below would be displayed in a Latin alphabet one week and Cyrillic the next. But they'd glean only so much to realize their world looked different from the one in the big city. They later learned their parents would never choose city life; there, people aged faster and died younger from the air pollution.

Their school teacher once told them they'd go on a trip to Belgrade to visit former President Tito's grave. When their parents heard of this, they immediately said no because their income was stretched thin already; they could not afford these luxuries. Selma and Mirza complained about it for a day or two and then their annoyance soon dissipated, distracted as they were by some childish game.

Selma and Mirza felt peaceful in each other's presence. Even when silently playing, they took comfort in knowing that a lack of words didn't imply any worries.

Selma had heard stories of how her mother could not conceive again after giving birth to her. She often caught her mother having sudden bursts of sadness or depression, unable to connect with her daughter or take any deep care for anything. Her hair would be unkempt, the depth of her eyes would grow by the day, and hoping to overturn it and make it disappear, she eventually went to the nearby mosque to talk to the imam and have him read her misfortune. He'd place a small pot above her head, and she'd looked down waiting for the sound of hot metal to meet the bottom of the pot, forming into its new shape that was her fear. The imam then read the shape and told her what her future looked like, reassuring her she had to be patient and have faith. He'd also suggest that she say certain prayers a couple of times a day.

Despite the encouragement from the imam, Selma's mother often said she felt like there was a demon in her body fighting to dominate, trying to steal her fertility forever. She was sick and tired of chasing her dreams, which she knew might never materialize. Her dream of having a son was becoming more and more faint, and wrinkles soon began to slowly build on her face and her bones slowly began to dissolve. As time moved on, her husband began to show less and less affection toward her, often lying in bed at night, turning his back to her, and falling asleep almost immediately. Selma would hear mother crying at night between her father's loud snores. She wasn't sure, but she thought she had heard her mother whisper the prayers the imam prescribed to her. At this point, she didn't care if she didn't give birth to a male. Any baby, a child, *her* child, whether it be a boy or a girl, was the new dream.

As if cast by a strange miracle, luck knocked on Aisha's door one day. The prayers came true. Or so she thought, anyway.

It was an early spring morning of 1991 when Selma woke up and saw her mother pack her purse with small necessities: her wallet—with Selma's photograph in the front—a few tissues, the prayer beads and her health insurance card. She took a few bills from the stash of money she kept hidden in her dresser and placed them in her bra, the most secure spot she had on her.

She took one final look in the purse to double check that she had her health insurance card and when she looked up, she caught a glimpse of herself in the mirror. She had a conspicuous smile on her face. But then it quickly turned into a worrisome grimace—she couldn't let herself be too happy just yet, not until her suspicion was confirmed at least.

The walk to the Doboj hospital was four kilometers —it would take about fifty minutes. Without available transportation in the village they lived in, she was used to walking everywhere, and as full of vigor and excitement as she was, she expected to walk it fast.

She walked into Selma's room where her daughter was still sleeping and gave her a quick kiss. Her only child, the daughter she loved so much that her heart could burst, would often snuggle up to her and caress her hands, on which the skin was coarse from the cold water she used to wash laundry in the well near the house. They were best friends. But lately, when her depression ensued, Aisha would push her away and look blankly at one spot as she tried to suppress her dark thoughts.

With the glimpse of hope, Aisha foresaw her happy self again, able to love, to give, to show the strength that seemed to have disappeared on her.

She walked out of the house and made her way to the Doboj hospital. The walk was tedious, much harder than she'd expected. She hadn't seen a soul the whole time, which was unusual, given the farm people liked to get up early to herd the sheep to the hills. She quickened her pace, ridden by anxiety. Before she had a chance to come up with questions for the doctor, she found herself standing in front of the small building with a worn-out sign saying *BOLNICA*—hospital. Her palms began to sweat and her heart was beating quickly: what if she was mistaken? Women missed their periods all the time only for them to return in an untimely fashion. It was possible she'd missed hers because she was so depressed and stressed, and her body was signaling that something was off.

The small office looked dark and uninviting and the walls were covered in someone's writing in Sharpie. The place smelled of anesthesia, remnants that would linger forever. Aisha sat on a chair in the waiting room with her toes touching the floor, her body positioned as if she was about to launch into the atmosphere. When the doctor's door opened, she quickly stood up, tightening the grip on her purse. A young woman came out.

"Mrs. Karic?"

"Good morning," she mustered, her voice cracking.

"Come on in." The woman signaled with her hand. "What brings you here today?"

"I missed my period," she stated bluntly, not knowing how to proceed now she was finally here.

"I see. When did you expect to get your period?"

"Two weeks ago. Is... is that a long time? Is it enough?"

"Well, we will see," the doctor said cheerfully. "I will send a sample of your blood to the lab for analysis and once I get the results, I will call you and let you know."

"Thank you." She paused. "You know, doctor. We've been trying many times. But no luck. I really hope this is it."

The doctor smiled.

"I hope so, too. You're still young. Women can rear children as long as they still get their period and they are healthy." She looked down her chart. "See, you are only thirty years old. That's still quite young. Do you have children already?"

"Yes. My dear Selma. She will be twelve in April."

"Wonderful. Now, why don't you roll up your sleeve so I can draw your blood." She took a needle and two test tubes from a small medicine cabinet in the corner, and then gently stabbed the needle into her arm. Aisha clenched onto her purse, closing her eyes to manage the pain.

"Done."

Aisha rolled down her sleeve and began to fidget. It was as if someone was rocking her back and forth, and she was trying to regain her balance.

"Doctor."

"Yes, Aisha."

"When do I find out?" The words came out in a near whisper and she could feel her palms begin to sweat again. Her belly seemed to tighten from the nervous ache.

"I will send your bloodwork to the lab as soon as we are done here, and I hope to call you in a few days."

"A few days," Aisha repeated.

"Yes, a few days. That's not a very long time."

That's what you think.

Those few days stretched like years, and as soon as she headed home the countdown began. At home, she wasn't quite herself. Putting herself to work as a distraction, she gathered hay into a stack, but the haystack didn't quite look like a cone—its shape resembled a small hill waiting for an up-rise.

She'd move slowly, daydreaming about the baby that she had tried to have for many years now. She'd see a tiny beautiful face in the haystack, and it'd smile at her, reaching out for her embrace and motherly warmth. When she picked apples, she'd see baby's head instead of the apple itself and would gently pick it, bring it to her face and caress it. Aisha would be constantly going to the house in the anticipation of a phone call, until one day the ring finally blasted through the house, sounding as if giant church bells were sending the sound waves vibrating through the square.

Her heart began to beat fast. What if this was the doctor?

"Aisha?"

"Yes?" Her voice trembled. She couldn't utter anything else.

"This is Doctor Hadzic. I am calling to let you know that you are pregnant."

Just as Aisha heard those words, the tension inside her subdued and she managed a big smile.

"Are... are you sure, doctor?"

"I'm quite positive. According to the results, you are four weeks gone. Congratulations. I will need you to come back in a couple of months. Take it easy now."

When Selma entered the room, she found her mother slamming down the phone receiver. Aisha had her face buried in her palms and her whole body shook. Selma wasn't sure if her mother was crying or laughing, and if she did either of those things, she wondered what prompted such an intense reaction.

"Mom, everything okay?" Selma spouted her words, reaching for her mom's hand to reveal her face. She saw her mother in tears, but they looked different this time; there wasn't a type of sadness associated with them like Selma had witnessed her mother before.

"Oh, dear." Her mom finally said. "I just heard the news from my doctor. You'll be a big sister soon."

"A sister? What... what does that mean, mom?" Selma never learned how a baby was brought into the world and what it meant.

"I'm pregnant. You will have a brother or a sister."

When Selma found out her mother was pregnant, she felt indifferent. When the baby came, she knew she would no longer be the center of her mother's universe. The thought haunted her at night, and she'd stare at the ceiling for hours, visualizing the small, new human occupying their space and lives. She'd picture her parents cooing to the baby, circling around it as if it were their most precious possession, something they would need to tend to constantly, while turning their back on her, ignoring her, as if she didn't exist. Selma would try to push the thoughts away and force herself to sleep by counting sheep—someone told her it worked—and by the time she'd count two hundred seventy-one, she'd finally fall into a deep sleep, an involuntary tear falling down her cheek.

As the months went by, Aisha's belly grew bigger and she no longer felt depressed. Her vigor and joy were quite apparent as she greeted her neighbors walking by their house, yelling out and waving to them.

"How are you today, Aisha?" a neighbor's voice echoed along the main village path.

"Never better. Come and have a cup of coffee. Let's catch up," she'd call back, inviting whomever walked by, even though they'd politely reject her invitation.

"I would, but I've got to run."

Aisha didn't seem to mind. As long as her world, the promise of it, was happy.

Nine months later, on an early winter morning, as icicles hugged the windows, she woke up with extreme pain in her stomach. Her contractions had begun. She woke up her husband gently and told him she was ready for the hospital. He jumped out of bed, slipped on the clothes nearest to him, and grabbed Aisha's arm to help to pull her out of bed. For she could barely move. Her stomach was as big as a house, and her feet were swollen, making her movements slow and exhausted.

His car was awaiting outside. Before they left the house, they checked up on Selma, who was sleeping in her bed. They grabbed a bag of things Aisha's doctor told her to prepare and they headed through the door.

Aisha was walking slowly through the snow in her worn-out ankle shoes; the snow was deeper than her ankles and she could feel the wetness seeping into the soles. But suddenly the wetness spread all over her legs, up to her crotch. Her water must have broken.

The car engine finally started on the fourth try, and they slowly made their way through unplowed snow to the hospital. The ride was slow, even though not a soul could be seen on the cold wintery morning.

Aisha felt the contractions increase with time. She held her stomach with her hands and prayed that she would make it to the hospital safe. Their car was known to suddenly stop and act out as if in a sudden burst of anger and spite. She only hoped that it would behave this time.

"Ahhh." She'd exhale and close her eyes to manage the pain.

"We're almost there, darling. Almost there."

When they arrived, he pulled her out of the car seat with great difficulty and grabbed her arm, placing it around his neck. He supported her as they walked through the hospital's hallways, yelling out for help.

"Anybody?! My wife is having a baby!"

A nurse came out of the surgery room and shushed him. "Sir, please do not yell. You'll wake up the patients."

Another nurse appeared pushing a wheelchair and helped Aisha into it before wheeling her into the surgery room. Her husband couldn't enter; it was the hospital's policy. But Aisha didn't think twice on whether she minded that or not. All she cared was that she would finally meet the precious little one and give him a hug and a kiss, sharing all the motherly love that she so wanted to.

As soon as she lay down on the hospital bed, she heard the cry. A healthy baby boy was born. Aisha herself began to cry. The tears wouldn't stop for a long time. The tears of joy. The tears of pain. The tears of relief. But she felt alive like never before.

Two days after the birth, Aisha was released from the hospital and sent home with her new son. He was born plump, a good eight and a half pounds. His cheeks were bursting with health; he'd coo and make noises. His nose looked like a cute button and his extremities were proportionate to his body. His cry was muffled and silent, the sound of a gentle little angel. Nearly perfect.

Before he was born, Aisha would think of names for days. If she had a baby girl, she'd name her Maida after her grandmother. But if she had a boy, most definitely she would name him Besim. When she looked at him, she'd see the name written with an invisible mark on his cheeks, and she was sure that he was born into the name.

Besim and Selma: her most valuable treasures. The

loves of her life that made her heart ache sometimes. And she'd silently cry in her handkerchief trying to compose her body and not show her trembles.

She'd expected Selma to be thrilled about their new family addition, but when she arrived home, Selma was nowhere to be found.

"Where is she?" she asked.

"She's in school, isn't she?" Adem replied.

"Today is Saturday. There's no school on Saturday."

"Oh, I lost track of the days. I saw her this morning. We had breakfast together."

The day her brother arrived, Selma found a spot to hide in their barn. It was so cold that tiny icicles were forming on the tip of her nose. She sat in a corner of the barn, crunched like someone had bent her in half, and stare at a spot, already reminiscing about the days when she was the center of the universe. Why should she love this baby? What was in it for her? But realizing it was her brother, she decided to give him a chance, to attempt to love him and be his rock.

A few days after his birth, the local imam showed up at their home to perform a circumcision. All of their family members showed up from nearby and afar to witness his first step into manhood. They all encircled the baby and the imam and watched with amused eyes as the ritual unfolded in front of them.

Selma sat between her parents, feeling bored, wanting all this to be over as soon as possible. But when the novelty of cutting through the skin began, Besim began to cry so hard that he nearly choked. His breathing stopped for a few seconds, and silence fell onto the room. Then the crying continued. The deep, loud voice echoed in the house, reaching Selma's ears in a most peculiar way. In it, she heard something more than a cry: a plea for help, a call for rescue perhaps.

Selma's eyes widened, and as she watched her brother in obvious pain she felt her hair stand on end. She felt her brother's profound innocence, his inability to defend himself, his failure to communicate his pain in a more intelligible way. Only loud, echoing cries. She wanted to jump out of her seat and reach for him. She looked at her mother on her right side, her father on her left, but they didn't seem to be alarmed at all. All she saw was the subtle smiles on their faces, making her feel a wave of relief. This moment was larger than her.

And in that moment she knew one thing only: from now on, she had to protect her brother from pain and suffering at all costs. She'd be the first one to give him a helping hand when he needed it, a kiss on a cheek when he needed love, a hug when he felt discomfort of any sort. She wanted to be his everything, larger than the Pacific Ocean, wider than the vast universe. She wanted to hold him in her arms and tell him he'd be all right. She was his big sister, and she better act like one.

As she made that resolve in her head, her days seemed lighter.

But the winter moved slowly and their days were filled with a bitter cold. Every once in a while, she'd over-hear the adults talking about the war in neighboring Croatia. They'd say that the Yugoslav Army turned against the Croats and that parts of the newly formed country were being ethnically cleansed. On the news, they'd show ravaged homes, burned bridges and people displaced, seemingly lost. Selma's father would usher her to bed as soon as her cartoons were over, leaving her to speculate what was on the news that he didn't want her to see. She knew he didn't want her to worry about the war. The war didn't concern them. It was far enough away, it wouldn't reach them. But often, she'd overhear her parents' conversation, which betrayed his calm.

"This looks bad, doesn't it?" Aisha would say.

"It sure does."

"The war won't come here, right?"

"It won't, it won't, don't worry."

When they speculated, Selma's father often told stories his father had told him from when he was a partisan soldier during World War II, fighting Nazis. In his squad were Muslims, Orthodox and Catholics, all united to fend the evil force. With the final victory of the war, Marshal Tito, the army commander, emerged as the winner, and built a country based on unity and brotherhood. All men were now equal, and everyone would more or less possess the same number of assets, thus making the country communist.

Selma's grandfather was a pious man who liked to visit the mosque on a daily basis to pray. He did it somewhat discretely, as he knew that the government of his newly created country, Yugoslavia, wasn't so keen on promulgating the organized religions. But he grew up going to a mosque at least once a day, and praying five times a day, for his parents taught him that praying would lead him to a more serene life. When he arrived at the mosque, he'd turn around to see if anyone saw him, remove his shoes at the door, and quickly disappear into his godly sacred space.

He'd eventually settled in Kotorosko near Doboj, a city north of the Bosnian capital. The new generations didn't care for religion as much. Selma's father learned all the prayers when he was a child, but he'd found that he'd rather get together with friends and neighbors and party with loud music and a strong plum alcoholic drink. His religion, Islam, didn't define him in his beliefs or values. He only cared to bring food on the table and live a quiet, decent life.

When the war raged in Croatia, the village kids began to play their own game of war. Mirza found a plastic gun in his parents' basement and summoned a few others from the village to join him in their game of pretend. They played an army of soldiers about to attack their enemy and Mirza would point at the trees and air, random places, and make noise—*pew pew*—and they'd run endlessly until they realized they were chasing nothing.

Whenever Selma caught a glimpse of the game she would shake her head.

"Why do you find these games interesting?"

"I don't know." He'd look at her, shrug his shoulders and drop his head down in embarrassment.

"Your war game is stupid," she continued. "You look like you're mad, blindly looking for something."

"Whatever." He combed his hair with his fingers and turn around to leave.

"Wait," she'd say. "Maybe you and I can make up our own game."

"Like what?"

"What if we pretend to be mom and dad and take care of our little baby." She held a large doll in her hand, bruised all over its body by a black marker. In her mind, she'd want to put herself in her parents' shoes to feel how it was to be a parent and be responsible for another life. Thus far, she had no sense of how an adult life worked. But playing the parent game with Mirza, she could get a glimpse of that world looked like and see if she liked it, if she ever could become a mother. Maybe the doll was ready for her love and affection. Maybe she could remove the markers soon and start the doll's life fresh and anew.

"Okay." Mirza responded quickly as if he welcomed a shift from playing the senseless war game.

"Do you think you would be a good dad?" Selma was testing the waters already, wondering about his ability to pull off an adulthood. More so, she was wondering if he ever had similar thoughts about becoming responsible for one's life. How would he feel about it?

"I don't know." Mirza shrugged his shoulders.

"I think you'd be a good dad." Selma wanted to enforce encouragement for Mirza to dig deeper and share with her. But it appeared that he hadn't given parenthood much thought at all so far. All he wanted was to play his games and be a boy.

"Oh yeah, how can you tell?"

"Because you listen to me," she said.

Mirza smiled.

"Only because I like you," he said. With that, Selma blushed and ran inside the house.

⬥

MEMORIES. THEY DIDN'T UNTANGLE SELMA'S PAST. They agitated her sleep; it became impossible, sporadic. In her scattered dreams, she'd see ghosts. They'd reach for her neck and try to strangle her. She'd try to escape and run away from them as fast as possible, but most times, her legs would give up. She'd fall to the ground and the ghosts would reach for her again, attack her, hoping to imprison her into their eternal life of nothingness in the void.

These dreams would wake her up in sweat and fear. She'd gasp, puffing for air. Every time she emerged from her nightmares, she could still feel the invisible hands around her neck. She often daydreamed about them, wondering on the ways she could rid herself of her burden, but it was always there on her shoulder, constantly. Her past memories haunted her, and she knew she'd never be able to push them away. They'd hang on, like a dreadful painting permanently attached to the wall.

Often when she was walking back from the store to her apartment, the same stray cat would follow her home. It was black with a white nose and a large white spot on its belly. Whenever she ran into it, the cat would meow, entangling itself between Selma's ankles, navigating around as if in a maze. Selma would try to escape its constant attention, but the cat kept following her, meowing as if asking for rescue. It must have been hungry.

Selma eventually let the cat enter her apartment and soon befriended her. The cat, who she named Spotty, made herself at home, after carefully checking out every corner of the apartment and sniffing everything she owned.

Slightly surprised at this, Selma looked for food right away: maybe she still had a can of tuna in the kitchen cabinet, or some leftover cheese in the refrigerator. When she placed down food, she was further surprised that she instinctually began to stroke Spotty. The cat would at first dodge her advances, seemingly frightened at her touch, but soon enough, when she sensed there was no danger, Spotty would cozy up to her legs and begin to purr.

The comfort was reciprocated, much for the fact that Spotty had no expectations of Selma. The only thing Spotty wanted was an occasional caress and a half-full bowl of food which she would devour in a matter of seconds. The stray cat would become Selma's daily companion, as long as Spotty minded her own business and left her alone.

Humans disgusted Selma. Her contempt for them grew each day. No other being could be so evil as a human. For when they killed or harmed their own, it was typically a conscious act. Humans were not like a hungry wolf or a tiger looking for prey to consume and survive. They performed horrors on their own kind. Would one wolf ever harm another wolf in such a way? Why did humans do so? She'd ponder these questions and most often wouldn't have an answer. Her bewilderment for human inhumanity was left unexplained. It only made her angry, and the more she thought about it, the more her anger grew into rage. Cats she could tolerate. Humans, she'd lost faith in. She doubted that they could ever be a truly altruistic and kind species.

February came and hinted longer days and warmer weather forthcoming with the spring. Selma arrived home one night after a seemingly long shift at the super-market. As usual, she'd turned on the TV to fill the silence. Spotty was nowhere to be found. She hoped that perhaps she was curled up in a safe space somewhere in the neighborhood.

She went to the bathroom and pulled out the hair tie from her hair, letting her long locks bounce free. Her interests didn't concern physical looks; she didn't think superficiality amounted to much and wouldn't advance one in life. She looked at herself in the mirror. Her eyebrows were long and wild, dangling over her big brown eyes. A colleague had recently asked her why she wouldn't pluck her brows, saying they looked bushy and un-womanly, but Selma simply shrugged, not looking at her, let alone replying. Comments like this one didn't bother her.

She looked at her nose, a bit flat, but nonetheless cute looking—like a button, as Mirza once said. She noticed two deep wrinkles hugging her nose on each side, the depth in which she hid her secrets and pain. She removed the scarf from her neck and she moved closer to the mirror to look at the long scar. *Will it ever heal?*

She raised her hand and slightly touched the red line and ever so gently caressed it, reminding her of its source.

In the corner of her eye, she noticed a drop of blood coming out of her nose, before landing on the white sink. She stared at the sink for a moment, watching as the drop soon turned into a small stream. Her nose was bleeding profusely.

"Not again."

She lifted her head and turned around to grab a piece of toilet paper, which she placed on the tip of her nose. Walking with her hand in front of her so as not to bang into the doors or furniture, she found her way to the bed and lay down, keeping her head lifted all the while.

The room was dingy, with only a bed and a small dresser placed against the wall opposite from her bed. That's all that had been there when she moved into the place. With a suitcase in tow, she didn't need anything else.

She looked to the ceiling and the old light which had three lightbulbs screwed in, but only one working. It occurred to her at first that she could ask Mirza to replace them, but she then quickly changed her mind. Selma learned not to mind things like this. As long as she could keep this one lightbulb on all the time, even when she was asleep, she would be fine. She hated darkness.

When her nose finally stopped bleeding, she got up from the bed and moved to the kitchen, walking through the living room where the TV was making its constant noise, a perfect distraction. With her meager salary, paying the higher electricity bill with the TV constantly on was a challenge, but she spent less money on food and it all seemed to balance out in the end. She opened up the fridge, and found a single bottle of ketchup, a couple of bottles of Coca-Cola and leftover meal from yesterday, uncovered. She stared at the food blankly for a few seconds, trying to concentrate and decide whether she was hungry enough to pick it up and eat it. She had never learned how to cook. She'd boiled an egg or two, once or twice, but nearly burned them, leaving them on the stove until all the water in the pot evaporated. When she did have food in the fridge, she'd leave it there for days and sometimes months. To her, food was mere nourishment. She'd eat only because hunger made her body hurt and she didn't want to deal with the discomfort.

Suddenly, though, as she was about to close the fridge door, she felt an immense sense of nausea and she belched. She held her hand to her mouth as if to stop herself from vomiting. But the nausea amplified when she noticed an old piece of chicken sitting on a fridge shelf. Her legs moved quickly to the bathroom where she bent down over the toilet and began to retch. A yellow liquid came out of her, nothing else. She propped herself back up and flushed the toilet. She spat a few times to make the liquid from her mouth dissipate.

She went back to the living room and lay on the

couch, curling herself into a small ball, with her knees bent up to her chin. The bitter taste in her mouth from vomiting made her cringe, but she did nothing to make it disappear. She fell asleep, as the cartoons were still running on TV.

A couple of hours later, she woke up as if someone was shaking her from a bad dream. She found herself lying across the couch. The clock on the wall showed ten at night. Early, much too early to go to bed. She grabbed her flip-on phone and found a message from Mirza:

Hey, beautiful, how was yr day???

She stared at the screen, and, as usual, flipped it shut, telling herself a reply could wait. Mirza was patient. He'd never force her to do anything. He had no expectation of her. He was *just there for her*. Her only human friend and companion.

When she woke up the following morning, her head felt groggy. Her nightmares extended into the day, for she always had them with her; she kept them inside. She took her anxiety pills and wondered whether there was any point in taking them.

Her phone rang. Mirza's name appeared on the screen. She ignored his call.

At work, she was welcomed by the suspicious eyes of her colleagues, who watched her as if she had dropped from a different universe. She got to work, moving the merchandise from the storage area to the shelves, minding her own business. As she walked down one aisle, the pregnancy tests caught her eye. She looked to her right then to her left, and when she realized no one was in her close proximity, she snatched one and stuffed it under her shirt. It wasn't that she couldn't afford it; it was just that she didn't want to be subjected to the numerous questions her colleagues would no doubt ask her, and be ridden by shame.

She ran to the bathroom and double checked the lock was indeed secured. She pulled down her pants, sat down, and positioned the stick between her legs. When she was finished, she threw the stick on the sink as if it were on fire and she didn't want to get burned.

Then she waited. A couple of minutes passed. Her nerves were getting to her. She was too nervous to grab the stick, for she wasn't quite sure what to expect. Could she have been pregnant? Her period hadn't come for a few months now. She tried to reflect on how pregnancy could happen; her memory wasn't her friend and it often failed her. Even if a faint of her memory hinted that she had sex, she couldn't remember when or how. The details had completely escaped her mind. All she knew was that the only person who could be the father was Mirza. He was the only person she'd ever been intimate with.

The stick was still sitting in the sink, and enough time had passed to get the results. Selma grabbed it and saw the two red lines. Not wanting to face what she knew that meant, she grabbed the box and double checked.

A strange sense of solitude came over her. When there was no doubt about it—she was pregnant—she put the stick back in her shirt and ran to go get her purse. She needed her pills.

Her heart was pounding and all she could see were

those two red lines in front of her eyes. She had to find a way to escape from Mirza and hide the baby inside her. She didn't want him to know that she had a baby, *his* baby.

All she could think was that the baby couldn't belong to her. She could never protect it.

❧ 3 ❧

UNITED STATES OF AMERICA

EMMA WAS SITTING IN HER OFFICE, BROWSING FOR houses on a real estate website, dreaming of what her new home could be. She always dreamt of living on a cute ranch, with three bedrooms, at least two bathrooms, a garage, a yard large enough for her children—she'd imagine running with them around the trees, a swing hanging down from one—and a large play area for them to enjoy.

Everyone kept saying the real estate bubble in the Boston area was about to burst. Houses would be more affordable. Brookline was her first choice; it would be an ideal town for them to live in. Having grown up in a similar Chicago suburb, she missed friendly neighbors chit-chatting in the morning across the picket fence, and people walking their dogs stopping by the curb to introduce themselves.

They could move to a suburb, but the commute

would be twice as long and stressful. Emma would often nudge Michael about the idea of buying a new house, especially now that the bubble burst was all the buzz, but he'd always try to knock some sense into her:

"Emma dear, I get it. You want a house where we can raise a family. But don't forget that we've got hundreds of thousands in school loans. Business school ain't cheap. I don't know how that's gonna look like to a mortgage company if we applied for a loan."

"My salary is higher now. That should help."

"Sure, but you didn't get the promotion that long ago. It takes a while to save up money for a down payment. We're looking at five per cent minimum. Still a lot of cash we don't have."

"I don't want to raise my family in our tiny apartment. This is not my idea of a family life."

"You just need to be patient. You want things to happen all at once. How about one thing at a time?"

As Emma looked at the houses on her screen, she cringed at the prices. What happened to her American dream? As she grew up, she was told that working hard would pay off someday, that things would fall into place and life would be good. She'd have a family, a big house with a picket fence, a car—maybe two—and enough money to spend on a vacation every year. Instead, all they had were hefty bills. Even though their Cambridge apartment was small and dumpy, it cost double the same place would elsewhere in the country. With their monthly rent, they could afford a mansion in Texas or Washington. And sure—they could choose to move, but they would not land jobs with high enough wages to pay off their school debt. Emma's patience was running thin. Overridden by the constant worry, she closed the web browser, trying to get the idea of buying a house out of her head.

She left the office around eight in the evening. Because her meetings took a lot of time during the day, she had no time to do her actual job. *Don't let this schedule become your norm.* Michael's words would often echo in her head. *Once you do, you'll never earn their respect.*

On her way home, she stopped by a local market in the corner of Central Square. She rarely visited this place, as she was a creature of habit. But, that evening, she walked in, feeling a little reckless.

"What lottery do you recommend I buy?" she asked the guy behind the counter. The man was missing a tooth and looked to be harassed by the constant lousy moods of his customers.

"Mega Millions. The next draw is tomorrow—two hundred million bucks."

"Okay. I will have one ticket." She reached for her purse to get her wallet out, then paused and looked up. "No, make it two. How much is a ticket anyway?"

"Two bucks." The man rolled his eyes.

"Two bucks. Can I have ten... ten tickets? Yes, I will have ten tickets please."

The man ran the cash register and handed her the tickets. Then, without even looking at her, he bid a good night.

Emma walked away hopeful. On her way home, she thought about all the possibilities if she won the lottery.

Two hundred million dollars. A lot of money. For one, she would pay off her student loans and it would finally feel like the degree she worked so hard for was finally earned. Next, she'd buy a house in a location of her choosing, all cash down, no mortgage. She'd make sure it was decked out in tasteful décor that highlighted the features: high ceilings, bay windows, a large eat-in-kitchen, the dining room for big family gatherings on holidays, a master suite with a Jacuzzi, a bath tub and a shower. With the money, she would help her parents and sister, and Michael's family as well. She could even afford that antique Cadillac her father had always yearned for. No one would ever worry any more.

Even if she won a million dollars, after the taxes were paid, she'd take home about six hundred thousand dollars. That much wasn't all bells and whistles, not in Boston anyway, but it was enough for a down payment on a house, furniture, and a car maybe.

Her rosy dreams were interrupted by a waft of marijuana that infiltrated her nostrils. It came from a couple of men sitting outside a bar. They were sitting on the ground with cardboards and blankets underneath them. Homeless. Emma would run into the homeless in Central Square quite often, and she'd wonder what happened for these men to lose their homes. Was it a tough job market? Mental issues? Drug and alcohol abuse? A combination? She couldn't imagine what it would be like if she or Michael lost their job. All their life plans would derail and her pregnancy plan would become nothing but a dream. The sight of the homeless reminded her that at least she had a home, as modest as her Cambridge apartment was.

She told Michael about the lottery tickets as he cooked dinner in the kitchen.

"That's lovely, darling," he said, coming up to her with a mitten in his hand and kissed her forehead.

As Emma heard Michael's sweet words of encouragement, she thought how naïve she was in believing the possibility that she could win the lottery. The odds were not in her favor. The odds were rarely in her favor. She only knew to work hard to achieve her goals.

The next evening, she sat at the kitchen table as the Mega Million numbers were drawn.

First number, five. Null.

Second number, twenty-eight. Null.

Third number. Thirty-seven—on one ticket!

Fourth number, nine—two tickets, but not the same as the one with thirty-seven.

Fifth number. Seventeen. This confirmed her hopelessness.

Mega Ball number—zero.

And there went her chance of winning her dreams or anything at all. At least a consolation prize of two dollars, to pay for one of the tickets, would have been satisfying.

"Shitbird," she whispered and went to bed.

They never lost sight of their mission to conceive. It was somewhat robotic and mechanical. After each time they tried, she'd whisper a little prayer to herself. She'd lift up her legs, under the pretense that this might help to usher the semen to her ovaries. She'd do anything to help with conception.

Days and months passed, and the results were always negative. As time went by, Emma fell into deeper despair. At work, she'd miss important meetings, often with Mary having to come to her office to remind her about them. When she'd finally enter the room, with a number of executives sitting around the oval table and sometimes even clients, Derek would give her a carefully measured look of disappointment. Her frustrated and fearful expression must have sent out a message that something was off in her life. She was not performing well at work at all.

The six months were up and Emma was still childless. At the moment she decided it was finally time to follow up with her doctor, she got a message from Derek to come see him in his office. *Here we go.*

Emma knew she wasn't being herself lately. She knew that she wasn't giving her best at work and that Derek must be gravely disappointed at his decision to give her a promotion.

She was prepared for the talk. She'd only listen this time, since she had no speech prepared in her defense or an explanation that might make Derek sympathize with her.

When she walked into his office, she found him sitting at his desk, his brows furrowed and a serious look on this face. He had his hands crossed over his lap, which he uncrossed to gesture to the seat opposite.

"Sit down," he said. "I think you know why I have

called you in. About seven months ago, I entrusted you with one of the most crucial roles in our company. You started off quite well, with full steam and enthusiasm, but lately, you seem to be veering off. And, quite frankly, I'm a bit taken aback. I trusted you could do the job. What happened?"

Silence ensued, as Emma didn't know how to respond. She felt guilty for her performance, but his words sounded empty. She wanted to open up and tell Derek everything that had been on her mind, everything that was happening in her life lately, but she also knew he'd probably find her unprofessional, a complainer of sorts, excuses to rationalize her poor performance.

In school, they taught her to use her business acumen wisely when it came to rising up. *Politics. Play the game*, was something someone had once told her. As a woman, she'd have to be careful about what words she chose or who she associated with. She'd been told many times not to appear too ambitious but to take a stand on issues... and to speak clearly and loudly so her message came across. To not show her emotions. Ever. Or her career might be ruined and she'd fall off the ladder before she'd even started to climb it.

She couldn't afford to lose her job. In a way, she lost a sight of what it meant to maintain a good job, to have the benefits, and to secure her future for a little one to come into her life. Her priority was etched in stone, like the only important mission in life she'd set herself onto. She had to become a mother no matter what. Derek wouldn't understand any of this, she'd assume. Regard-

60

less, she knew that leaving Derek in silence would make it much worse. She'd better say something.

"I'm so sorry. Yes, I'm working on some personal stuff at home, and I haven't been myself lately. It's not that I don't care about the company or my job—I actually love my job—but the things I've been dealing with have been stressful. I'm sorry if you feel I am a disappointment."

Silence fell upon them again, and Derek looked at her with wide eyes. It was as if he didn't expect an honest admission from her to her own failure.

"Emma! You can't just say you're sorry. I get you're stressed out. But isn't *everyone* these days? The stakes are high, for crying out loud." He banged the fist on his table, making Emma jump in her seat. She had never seen him this angry. "This is embarrassing. I can't even *imagine* what the board of directors is saying. I'm waiting for the call and I know it won't be pleasant. If the call ever comes, I'll need to be prepared. Prepared. Do you know what that means?"

"I have no idea. I could only guess." In Emma's mind, anything was possible. But she couldn't explain what was happening to her lately. Her memory worsened and she seemed quite absentminded, as she kept forgetting important meetings and deadlines. All this could possibly lead to her losing her job, or getting demoted, but she kept faith that things would ultimately work themselves out. She could find another high-paying job with great benefits, and she'd be on her way to fulfilling her dream of giving the life her child deserved. Everything was fixable. Almost everything.

Nothing could be worse than not being able to become a mother.

"If I get the call, Emma, we go back to square one. I'll need to take the title away, and that also means taking the money away. The next person in line would be more than happy to step up and really earn it."

Earn it. The words rang in Emma's mind. What did it take to earn things in life? And even if you earned something, it just meant one more thing you could lose anyway. It was pointless.

When she came home that day, she told Michael nothing. With his usual even keel attitude, he'd offer the same question he always did. "How was your day, sweetheart?"

"Fine."

"Just fine?"

"Yes, just fine." She didn't want to offer a more expansive response.

"Hey, everything okay?"

"Everything okay? No, no, nothing is okay!" she snapped. "It's been six months already, and I am still not pregnant."

"What do you want me to do about it?" Michael's face appeared puzzled, surprised at Emma's reaction. He knew Emma could flare up easily when things didn't go her way, but he had never seen her so exasperated.

"How about not forget about it, for starters?"

"I didn't forget about it! Emma, we talk about having kids all the time. And I mean, all the time. First thing in the morning, texting during the day, last thing before bed, even during sex! You really think I would forget?"

"Then, then... at least show you care, damn it!" She was screaming from top of her lungs and her face was covered in tears. It became evident that her promotion at work started to take a toll on her. Too many hours of meetings and sitting in front of her computer consumed her entirely. She had no time to pause and think of herself and her needs. Deep down, she knew Michael wasn't to blame for her stress level, but he was the easiest target to blame.

Michael approached her and enveloped his arms around her shaking body, caressing her hair with one hand.

"Sweetheart, my goodness." He squeezed her tightly as she hyperventilated. "It's not over yet. We have other options. There's always IVF. Remember what the doctor said?"

He held her tight while she shivered in his arms. They stood like that, in their kitchen, for a good five minutes until Emma came to her senses.

"Let's call the doctor tomorrow. I guess IVF it will be," she declared. "We should start the process as soon as possible."

🍂

WITH THE DECISION CAME A NEW WAVE OF HOPE. Emma's dream of becoming a mother was getting closer to reality. Her burning desire to have children was born when she herself was a little child. She didn't get too many gifts back then, but when her paternal grandmother, Gretchen, gifted her a doll on her fifth birthday, it became her most precious possession. This doll—she took it everywhere with her. She'd place her next to her in bed and caress her fake hair, pretending it was alive. She'd make up stories and tell them to the doll, hoping she'd enjoy them. The doll looked as if it was from another, much earlier era. The head was too big for the rest of the body, the hair was in disarray, and her simple outfit was made of cheap fabric. Emma still had that doll; it looked down on their bed from where it sat on a shelf. Michael would sometimes mention how creeped out he was by the doll. More often than not, they'd laugh about it, but Michael knew: the doll wasn't going anywhere.

Over time, their friends began to grow families. Her female friends would glow as their bellies grew and all they talked about was the nausea they felt in the morning and what color they'd paint their nurseries. When her friends shared their baby-related stories, Emma's mouth would twitch from envy. She'd bite at her lip so as not to reveal the angst.

When they were born, she'd go for a visit, pick them up and secretly smell them. She'd inhale the baby's breath as she held them tight, imagining it was her own. The baby would coo in her embrace, place their head on her shoulder and look at her longingly. Emma would smile, but behind that smile was a deeply rooted pain.

She felt relieved to know that she had the option of becoming a parent. She had heard that the probability of getting pregnant with IVF was high. She couldn't wait to call the doctor's office.

Immediately the day after she and Michael decided to try IVF, she picked up the phone, ready to make the request. Emma was sitting at her desk at work, watching clouds form above the Cambridge skyline. The transition from fall to winter in Boston seemed unexpectedly swift, and she could feel long cold days coming.

She heard the voice on the other line. "This is Dr. Johnson's office, how may I help you?"

"Hi, I need to speak with Dr. Johnson."

"She's with a patient now. Can I take a message?"

"Well... it's been six months and we have not conceived yet. We're ready for the next steps."

The receptionist's voice became much softer. "I'll be sure to let Dr. Johnson know."

When Dr. Johnson called a few hours later, she offered no words of empathy at the news that Emma and Michael had still been unsuccessful. Abruptly, she informed them that for the IVF procedure, they'd need to contact a fertility clinic.

"She sounded so cold." Emma told Michael when she arrived home that evening. "Or maybe I heard it that way, because I've been frustrated with everything."

"I bet this wasn't her first time. She's probably used to it."

At this, Emma felt relief. She wasn't the only one dealing with this burden.

A few days later, Michael was driving them to the fertility clinic a few towns over. Emma sat in the passenger seat motionless, watching as the houses became a blur. She was still daydreaming of becoming a home owner, taking a step forward in realizing her life fulfillment, completing her lifelong milestones. What did it take to earn a home? Hard work? Less debt? A draw of luck?

"Emma? Are you listening?" Michael's annoyed tone distracted her.

"What?"

"I was telling you a story about my buddy back home who's getting married. I asked you if you wanted to go. It's in September."

"Depends. It all depends."

Michael didn't even need to ask. Emma was entirely consumed by her plan on becoming a mother; she made it clear that all minor plans were ancillary and unimportant. Motherhood was her number one goal.

"I see."

They arrived at a long and tall brick building that housed the fertility clinic. The drab exterior of ruined façade in the building corner and dark windows would deter most from entering. Even Emma made a face when she saw it. *The rent must be cheap.* But the friendliness of the receptionist made up for the dreary look of the outside. They were ushered to a room with a single bed and a chair on one side, and a sink on the other. They waited for several minutes, in complete silence, until the doctor, a short Asian woman, knocked the door and came in.

"Hi, I'm Doctor Huang." She extended her hand to

TILL A BETTER WORLD:

shake theirs, and offered a smile. Her friendliness put Emma at ease. "Tell me more as to why you're here."

"We'd like to have a baby as soon as possible."

When Dr. Huang smiled at her sweetly, Emma realized how naïve she sounded.

"Indeed. I can help with that. Let me explain how in vitro fertilization, or as we call it IVF, works."

Emma rolled her eyes in her mind: *yes, I know what IVF stands for.* Immediately after, Emma put a smile on her face to counteract her reaction. She was surprised to learn how impatient and intolerant she was becoming. To shake off her negativity, she propped herself up in the chair and began to listen to Dr. Huang intently about the procedure. As the information traveled to her ears, she nodded to acknowledge its importance and to show she was present.

The procedure sounded tasking, but nonetheless not impossible. Always picturing the image of her with a big belly, she had no problems with any of the steps Dr. Huang carefully explained to them.

"And now comes the most painful part." Dr. Huang offered another smile that quickly disappeared. "I looked up your health insurance, and it doesn't look like it will cover all the expenses for the procedure."

"It doesn't?" Emma was surprised. She somehow thought that working for a good company would have enough benefits to cover this.

"No. Unfortunately, health insurance companies do not deem unnatural conception critical. You'll have to pay a good portion out of your own pocket. But the good news is, you can finance with the clinic for a low monthly interest rate."

Suddenly, Emma felt she was in a car dealership, not at a place that should care about her and her well-being.

"That's good news." Michael said, sounding all business-like. "Before we commit to any procedures, we will need to discuss all of our options here."

"Yes, of course," the doctor said.

"How much are we talking about here?" Michael made a gesture that looked as if he were opening a jar.

"Well, a typical procedure goes into twenty, twenty-five thousand dollars. That's the out of pocket amount, on average."

Another shocking surprise. Emma felt like she was washed ashore. The waves kept splashing her and weighing her down, the rip current pulling her under the water. Why could nothing ever be easy?

She and Michael rode back in silence. All Emma wanted to do was go home, but she needed to go into work, where another turbulent day awaited her, one that would further sabotage her new job.

Michael interrupted the silence. "Twenty-five thousand dollars. Holy shit, right?"

Emma jerked her head to take a look at him. His eyes were big and wide, his face awash with bewilderment and fear.

"I heard Dr. Huang. What about it?" She couldn't let Michael's fear seep into her psyche. With all her might, she needed to remain strong, to be the voice of reason.

Michael was overreacting, she thought. Now was not the time to proclaim worries and doubts.

"It's a lot of money," Michael said.

"It is. But we won't be backing out from our plan." Emma kept her reassurances with the voice sounding soft and confident at the same time.

"Yeah. Yeah."

Emma could sense the skepticism in his voice. "What's that supposed to mean, Michael?"

"Nothing."

"Are you saying you no longer want kids?" Emma said. She was trying hard not to be affected by Michael's fears.

"That's not what I'm saying at all."

"What then?" Emma asked.

"Well, where do we come up with all that money?"

"If there's a will, there's a way, you know how they say it." She smiled to ease the situation. She placed her hand on his leg and gently rubbed it. He looked down from the wheel quickly and Emma removed her hand, thinking Michael didn't want to be touched at that moment.

"Really? That's what they say? What are you—in the la-la land?"

"Screw you, Michael. I don't want your negativity right now." Another reaction she didn't expect. She needed to remain strong no matter what.

"It's not negativity. It's a simple question—where do we get that much money."

"I'll figure something out, don't worry."

When she arrived at the office, she stormed out of the car and slammed the door.

Emma came up with a plan. Self-reliance and perseverance were the qualities she needed to demonstrate to herself. Over her lunch break, which she felt guilty for taking since she had been late in that morning after the doctor's appointment, she left the office, crossed the street and found herself in front of a familiar bank. She stood there for a few seconds, looking at her reflection in the window. She saw herself as a child, the little Emma, lying in bed, while her mother stroked her hair as she tried to coax her to sleep. She remembered the unsolicited piece of advice her mother had often given her and Belinda. She'd tell them never to give up on a cause worth pursuing, even if they had to take a risk. She'd tell them not to fear, that fear was often the thought stopper and was what prevented them from reaching their dream. Before Emma was even old enough to understand what death was or what it entailed, her mother would preach how life was too short and that if the present wasn't used to propel our dreams, then our dreams would always stay in the past, behind us.

She walked through the bank's front door and found herself in a lobby where the smell of fresh paint wafted through the air. The fact that everything seemed new—furniture, paint on the walls, carpet, the unscratched plexiglass in front of each teller—gave her the courage to proceed with her plan.

She was approached by a young man in a suit and asked her how he could help.

"I made an appointment earlier today with Charles."

"Ah, yes. Please follow me."

They walked several feet until they arrived in a corner office. A younger man, wearing a suit and a tie, hair carefully combed to the side, and a moustache on his square face sat at a desk. He lifted his head from where he had been focused in a notebook. When he saw Emma at the door, he stood up.

"Please come in. Sit down." She moved forward hesitantly as if she was about to enter a trap. "It's quite a pleasure to meet you. What can I do for you today?"

"I would like to apply for a loan." She whispered, unsure of her own words. Another loan piling on her existing debt sounded like a bad idea. But it was her only choice.

"What kind of loan, Mrs..."?

"Mrs. Harris."

"Mrs. Harris. Before we consider this, I need to ask you if you are already a customer with the bank," Charles said.

"No, no I'm not. Is that a problem?" *Oh no.* The fear of her application being rejected materialized quickly. Staying calm through this conversation was important more than ever. Emma couldn't let her imaginary predictions become self-fulfilling prophecy. She couldn't let Charles smell her fear.

"No, not a problem at all." Charles laughed softly. "I will need your driver's license and social security number to get started."

"Yes, absolutely." She'd comply with any request. She heard her mother's voice whispering in her mind, *take the risk for a goal worth pursuing. Be in the now.*

"And of course, I will need to check your credit score before we open an account with the bank for you."

"Sure." Emma looked through her purse to get her driver's license and she jotted down her social security number on a scrap of paper.

"I must warn you that your loan will depend on your credit score. How much money do you need to borrow, Mrs. Harris?"

"I don't know. About fifty thousand dollars." Of course, she imagined this amount would secure their plan if more than one round of procedure was needed.

Charles's shoulders slumped down, as if he just heard the worst news. But he didn't say anything to suggest this.

"Let me see what I can do for you." He looked down her driver's license and began to type on his keyboard. His brows furrowed as he concentrated on the task. "Mrs. Harris, you know you could submit an application for a loan online, right? It's a new way of doing business these days. Technology."

"Yes. Yes, I am aware. But I'm old fashioned." As she said those words, she cringed. Old fashioned was never her style.

Charles went back to typing, finishing by hitting the last key pronouncedly as if he were ending a piano concerto.

"Are you looking to have a co-signer on the loan?"

"No. It's just me."

"Well, Mrs. Harris, I just ran your credit score. It is not the best, but it's not the worst either. I see you have student loans that are quite high." He leaned forward to look at the screen more carefully. "And one of your credit cards has a high balance. In order for the bank to consider giving you a loan, I'd need to speak to our general manager first."

"That's fine. Do what you need to." She waved her hand at him to gesture how insignificant this step might be, even though she knew it could prove to be detrimental to getting a loan.

"Unfortunately, he is out of the office now, but I will speak with him later this afternoon and inform you of his decision. If he is in agreement, I'll have you submit an application, online or here at the bank—whichever you prefer. I will also need get a copy of your two most recent paystubs as proof of your income. Hopefully you hear from me with the good news." He managed a smile again. She saw it as a good sign. She smiled back and thanked him for speaking with his manager.

When she returned to the office, a pile of paperwork awaited her. She was unmotivated to tackle it, so she opened up a web browser and tapped into the search engine:

IVF probability

Within seconds, a slew of search results appeared. With the top result came an astonishing surprise. There was only a thirty per cent chance of getting pregnant per cycle. And with each cycle, the probability went down while the cost went up. As Emma learned this information, she felt empty inside, depleted. She felt dizzy. She leaned back against the chair and closed her eyes to help calm herself.

The phone ringing startled her. She looked down her watch and saw it was one twenty. She wondered who might be calling her. As of late, she hadn't received too many cold calls. She hesitantly picked up the phone, "Hello."

"Hello, is this Emma Harris?"

"Speaking." She couldn't recognize the voice on the other line.

"This is Thomas Rilley with the Rilley Associates." *Shit*, Emma thought. The second she heard his name, she realized that she had forgotten to deliver an important analysis for product sales. The Rilley Associates was the biggest client in her portfolio and Derek gently reminded her to be extra sensitive to their needs, as their collaboration could become lucrative in the long run.

"Oh hi, Thomas. How are you?" But Thomas wasn't interested in the niceties.

"I'm calling to express my disappointment in your service. I've been trying to reach you via email and phone, but all of them have remained unanswered."

"I am very sorry, Thomas. I have a perfect explanation for that."

"I'm sure you do. When do you think you can deliver the folio?"

"Umm. I will do my best to do it by the end of this week."

"Tomorrow?" *Shit. Tomorrow is the end of the week.*

Emma didn't realize how time moved quickly when life became a whirlwind.

"Tomorrow, or Monday noon at the latest."

"Make that tomorrow." His voice was stern. Before she could reassure him she was on it, he had already hung up.

Emma slouched on her chair and closed her eyes. Her chest was feeling a bit heavy, and she started to breathe heavily to calm down and center herself. Her life had become a mess lately, and if she lost this most promising client, her job could be at stake. With the job loss, she could bid her pregnancy goodbye. She couldn't afford a comfortable life for a baby with only Michael's salary.

Getting a loan was as important as ever now. But from the sound of the bank officer, she wasn't sure she'd qualified for it. Her credit score was not up to par, her debt was way too high, and she was a single applicant. If she had roped Michael into this, perhaps they had a better chance together. But she didn't think Michael was averse to the risk like she was. When she spoke about the costs, he sounded too alarmed and worried that money would present the biggest obstacle in their becoming parents. But Emma wouldn't let that obstacle deter her from plan. If her loan idea didn't pan out, she would find a way to pave in the certainty of becoming a parent.

The phone ring disrupted her deep thoughts. This time, her cellphone rang, and she jumped out of her chair. It was the phone number she did not recognize.

Who could it be? She stared at the phone for a second and the curiosity made her answer.

"Hello?"

"This is Charles from the bank."

Emma took a deep breath in anticipation. This was it.

"I'm calling to share the good news. I spoke with the general manager earlier, and it looks like we will most likely be able to get you a loan. Just let me know how you'd like to fill out the application."

"How much can I borrow?" she asked, jumping to the most important question.

"We will need to determine that once we get your application. However, based on my conversation with our general manager, fifty thousand may not be possible."

"Wh... why? My income is decent."

"I get that, but your credit score is quite not up to par. You have too much debt."

Emma's head began to spin again. The price of education should not be at the price of a life.

"I'll take whatever you offer. I'll come by the bank tomorrow."

☙❦❧

ONE THING EMMA DESPISED WAS LIES. WHEN SHE WAS growing up, and her dad came home drunk, he would tell her mother that he'd been with his colleagues when they all knew that was all by his lonesome. Her mother would never question him, at least not in front of the children, but Emma could sense, even at a young age, her father's lies. Who went out for a happy hour and got wasted? With their colleagues, no less?

But one thing Emma knew was that at times lies were meant to protect someone, intentionally or not. Now that her world was upside down, black turned white and white turned black, she indulged in her own world of deception.

In the evening, when she arrived home, she found Michael in an unusually unsettled mood: he was sitting at his computer with furrowed brows; no typical smile or kiss to greet her, no dinner cooking in the kitchen.

"Hi, honey." She tried to balance out his mood as she greeted him.

"Hi." He did not look up from his computer.

"What's going on?"

He looked up straight at her. "I can't stop thinking about what Dr. Huang told us. Twenty thousand dollars per cycle. Do they all think money grows on trees?"

Emma smiled, a sign of relief.

"I have some good news to share." *This won't be easy*, Emma thought. She felt guilty about the message she prepared to deliver, but in the larger scheme of things, she thought it was one way to put Michael's concerns at bay and to go on with her plan.

"You do?"

"Yeah. I called my mom today." She paused and Michael lifted his brow, anticipating her next words. "I told her about what the doctor said and the cost of the procedure. She said she'd lend us money."

Emma couldn't stop smiling.

"Really? Your mom?"

"Yes. Why is that so surprising?" She was concerned that her lie would be discovered right off the bat. But this was the point of no return. She had to continue the deception.

"Your mom a teacher, and your dad a car salesman? Where did they get that kind of money from?"

"I know. She said they'd been saving all these years for 'just in case'." She made the quotation mark gesture with two fingers of each hand.

"I don't feel comfortable taking your parents' money," Michael said.

"What? Why? They're my parents, and they want us to be happy."

"Yeah, I get it. It just doesn't seem like a good idea. I'd rather take out a loan than borrow from them."

"You would?" Emma widened her eyes. Her feelings of guilt about lying to her own husband sprouted fast. She bit her lip and furrowed her eyebrows, hating the situation she got herself into. Maybe she could have avoided it if she had been less skeptical about Michael's doubts.

"Yeah. Can't be easy for your parents. Although, getting a loan is probably not that easy either these days."

Emma let out a sigh of relief. She moved toward him and hugged him around his waist.

"Honey, I think we should take it. It would really make my parents happy if we did. Then we can call the fertility clinic and start the process." She looked him in the eyes and for the first time noticed fear in them. She gave him a smile to ease his feelings. "Don't you think?"

"Okay. I trust you on this. We'll find a way to thank them."

Emma kept silent.

That night, she couldn't force herself to sleep. Her lie gnawed at her and she kept thinking of who she had become. Her father? Was she becoming an addict herself, drunk in her desire to be a mother? Could she no longer sense the reality, decipher her emotions that made her do things out of the ordinary? However she felt, her mother's words would always elbow themselves through the whirlwind and override any other feeling: *fight for the good cause no matter what.*

And with that thought, Emma watched the sun rise above the tree line out her bedroom window. As the sun finally appeared in all its glory, she closed her eyes and fell into deep asleep.

Exhausted from a lack of sleep, Emma slept in, ignoring her alarm. She snoozed it once, twice. When the alarm went off for the third time, she opened her eyes, looked at her phone and realized she was late for work.

Michael, who was an early riser, had already left.

When she stepped into her office, Derek was sitting at her desk, taking her by surprise. *Can he do this, invade my space,* was the first thought that crossed her mind.

As she bid him a good morning, he looked at his watch, raised his eyes and said:

"Well, it's almost afternoon."

"Is it?" She didn't know what else to say.

"I'm afraid so. I didn't hear from you that you were running late. Is there a reason for such negligence?"

Negligence? More like an oversight.

"I am very sorry. I wasn't feeling well, so I slept in. I will definitely call next time."

"I think that's a great idea. Consider this a verbal warning, Emma. One more, and I'll have to take action, and you know what that means." He stood up and walked out the door, quickly disappearing from Emma's sight.

She didn't bother to start work. She did not sit down at her desk nor check her email. Instead, she placed her computer bag on the chair, fixed her coat, and walked through the door. Seconds later, she found herself across the street again, walking into the bank. The same person as yesterday greeted her and asked her what he could do to help.

"Yes. I'm looking for Charles. He asked me to come in and fill out a loan application."

"Sure, absolutely." He beamed with enthusiasm. "Follow me."

❦ 4 ❦

BOSNIA AND HERZEGOVINA

SELMA DISLIKED DOCTORS. WHEN SHE WAS LITTLE, HER mother would take her to the Doboj hospital for a yearly check-up, and the trip was so long and tedious, especially for such a short visit. The doctor would check her lungs with a stethoscope so cold it made her jump off her chair. She would then have Selma open her mouth and put a wooden stick inside to check her throat and tonsils. She'd poke and prod the rest of her body, looking for any deformities and deficiencies, never ever finding any.

When she turned seven, the doctor finally declared something was wrong: her tonsils had to be taken out and Selma needed to be hospitalized. Dank and smelling of anesthesia, the hospital was anything but pleasant, and when she woke up from the surgery, her throat was dry. It felt as if someone had reached down her throat and pulled her organs out. She couldn't talk, she couldn't eat. She felt sick for days, and she took long naps during the day until the anesthesia wore off. She recalled her mother sitting by her bed and caressing her hair.

Ever since the tonsil surgery, Selma told her mother she'd never see a doctor again.

"What if you get sick?" Her mother asked her, amused.

"I will never get sick," Selma replied.

"You don't go to a doctor only when you're sick."

"You don't?"

"No. When you grow up and become a woman, you will want to see a lady doctor."

"But the doctor we saw last week was a lady doctor." Her mother laughed.

"True. A lady doctor is a special kind. It's the kind that takes care of women. They're there to help you have a baby. When you grow up, and have a husband."

"A baby? Who says I want to have a baby?" She was an only child then, immensely comfortable in the world of full attention from her parents. She couldn't imagine another human being occupying her life.

"Oh, you do. There's nothing better than being a mother." Aisha smiled at her.

"And what if I don't want to?"

"Oh, you do, you will."

Selma tried to recall the last time she had intercourse with Mirza. She couldn't remember when it happened exactly, for, most of the time, she'd dodge his advances and tell him she wasn't ready. Until it did happen one day —the day she moved into her new apartment. But she now deeply regretted it. She was not meant to be a mother, not a good mother certainly. And if she couldn't be a good mother, then she didn't want to be one of any kind. If she could only recall when she had last lain with him, she would know when approximately she conceived. But most memories failed her, and she couldn't remember at all.

She recalled her mother's words about being pregnant and going to see a lady doctor, one that helped deliver babies. Maybe it was a time to make an appointment and find out when she would be due.

Her only mission was to hide this pregnancy from Mirza. She would never become a mother, regardless of his wishes. Her decision was made swiftly and easily: the instant she saw the doctor, she would proclaim the baby unwanted. She'd say she wanted an abortion, and nothing would persuade her to keep this child. After all, it was her body and nobody else could interfere in her decision making.

Ever since Mirza had returned to her life after the war, her relationship with him morphed into a strange and unwanted form. They had been so close when they were little, but a huge gap of time and space now separated them. When the Bosnian War began, Selma and Mirza had lost their connection; she had no idea what had happened to him and whether he was still alive. According to the rumors, his whole family escaped Kotorsko early spring morning of 1992 and found themselves north across the border, ending up in Germany as refugees.

But their reunion was one that came unexpectedly.

When Selma arrived in Sarajevo shortly after the war ended, she happened to run into him on the main street. They'd walked toward each other, staring, disbelieving that they were reunited, still alive. Mirza looked giant and tall. He had grown from a sweet teenage boy into a mature, robust, and serious man.

They'd both stopped in their tracks and Mirza finally exclaimed: "Selma! Is that you?"

"Mirza?" she called out and ran to him.

He squeezed her hard in a hug, and Selma could feel him shivering in the embrace. She pulled back and saw a tear falling down his cheek.

Yet Selma felt indifferent about their encounter. She was glad to see Mirza was still alive, but that was the extent of her happiness.

Selma could never forget Mirza's sudden disappearance without saying goodbye to her. The war had just started, and people began to panic and move about. Along with his family, he found his way to a safe place the day before the dreadful infiltration of the enemy took place in Kotorsko. Where was Mirza when Selma ran and ran that early morning to save her life and escape the evil? Perhaps, it wasn't his fault for disappearing so suddenly, but he could have stopped by her house for a few minutes to tell her he was leaving. To tell her he was running for safety and advise her and her family to do the same. But the coward in Selma's mind that he was, he chose to leave—leave their friendship behind like it never existed.

"How have you been? Let's go and get a cup of coffee

if you have time." He was still shivering slightly, looking at her as if he was looking at a goddess.

"Sure, I have a few minutes." They walked to a nearby coffee shop in complete silence. What they had during their childhood was no longer felt, no longer existing between the close friends they once were. Selma chose his occasional company out of familiarity, but the cowardly image of him stayed with her and propelled her back to solitary life.

They sat down, and Mirza, holding the same intense stare, began to speak.

"Selma. I can't believe this is you. You have changed so much." He reached for her hands, but she pulled them away from his quickly. "I tried to find you during the war, but whatever clues I had led me nowhere. I didn't know if you stayed in Kotorsko or what might have happened to you and your family. So, tell me, what are you doing here, in Sarajevo?"

She shrugged, and simply said, "I don't know." She didn't feel particularly enthusiastic or interested in sharing with Mirza. If he had been so caring, he would have chosen to see her before he escaped Kotorsko.

"Are you with your parents? How's your brother? He must be big by now." She looked at him with the eyes enraged, penetrating Mirza's. This time, the silence seemed long and painful. Mirza began to fidget in his seat, looking beyond Selma as if seeking an escape.

"I don't know. I don't know what happened to my parents, where they are. They may be alive. Or not. All I heard was they were displaced."

Mirza shook his head in disbelief. "I heard our villagers were taken by some paramilitary Serbian groups in early March. Is that true?"

"Yeah, probably." Selma lowered her head. She didn't want to look Mirza in the eye. She didn't want to tell the story of the morning the soldiers took over their village. "I'm still looking for my parents. I heard you were in Germany."

"Germany? I wish. I was in Sarajevo the whole time. We tried to leave the country but a couple of days after we arrived the city was blocked-in and then the Serbs besieged the city. We were trapped here the entire war."

Selma was surprised to hear this. It was at that point she realized that she shouldn't have believed everything she heard. She also realized that truth during the war was always a bit stretched. She was quite certain she didn't trust anyone.

"Where do you live?" he asked.

"Over there." She pointed west, where the orphanage house was located.

"Where?"

"I live in the orphanage house."

The orphanage was built shortly after the war, when it was realized that too many children were left without parents, with no one to care for them. When Selma arrived in Sarajevo, she'd rang the doorbell on the main gate where a friendly man greeted her. They took her in and noted her personal information. When asked why she was there, she explained that she didn't know where her parents were. She needed help to find them. They asked her for leads, but all she could muster was a tid-bit about the dreadful morning the two men invaded her home and took her family away.

Mirza couldn't hide his surprise. "Seriously?"

"Yeah. I had no place to go when I came here."

After their encounter, Mirza came to visit Selma at the orphanage more often. He'd scheme on how to get her out of there, so she could live a more independent life, residing somewhere he could frequent so he'd become close to her again. Through Mirza, who appeared so inquisitive with the orphanage staff, Selma learned that since the age of eighteen, she had been eligible to move out and get her own apartment that the city would secure. In fact, it was the orphanage's policy that the children had to move out once they became adults and ready. He'd met all the key players in the orphanage and made himself at home, comfortable enough to convince them to appoint him Selma's guardian even though they were the same age.

On the day he discovered she could be freed from the orphanage he went to her, eagerly.

"You know you could get an apartment on your own. You're old enough now and you can leave this terrible place. I can help you situate yourself." Selma didn't know if calling it terrible was the right choice. It was good to her over the years, even though it never felt like a true home without a close-knit family.

Then one day, not too long after, he showed up at the orphanage with keys in his hands.

"Look what I have," he said as he dangled them in front of her face.

"Cool," she replied. "Thanks for making it happen." She smiled. She couldn't remember the last time she cracked a smile. She liked the idea of living alone, as she enjoyed silence and recluse.

They spent the next couple of days situating Selma in her new home. The apartment used to belong to a family that had left at the brink of war and never returned. Some of the furniture was still there, but it was marked with age and lack of use.

Mirza was acting as if it was the best day of her life. But Selma looked disinterested, grounded in this new reality. She walked around the apartment, carefully choosing steps as if someone was watching her from behind a corner. There was nothing special about the place. In fact, it looked uninviting, with brown drapes over dirty windows, and the kitchen needed a major overhaul. The stove was original—from the late seventies —and the fridge looked a bit wobbly, making a constant noise. But it was a home, as depressing as it seemed to her. She knew she wouldn't miss the orphanage and their demanding expectations of her to become friendlier to the other children there, or to be more connected to others. In her new home, she didn't need to answer to anyone. Being alone suited her the most.

Mirza didn't care about the house's appearance. He'd invite himself over often, too often for Selma's liking, and try to resume the connection they had once had as children. He was still stuck living with his parents, unable to afford an apartment of his own. He worked as a waiter, perpetually hopping from one coffee shop to another, changing employers, as they tended to shut down due to a poor location or a high competition. After the war, Bosnians had hoped to take on business opportunities and find a better way to make earnings and survive, but the economy was still fragile and many failed. As each coffee shop closed, Mirza would get even more frustrated. He'd start calling people frantically to find out if they know anybody who needed a waiter. With no education, that was his only choice. He was a peasant in his blood and that fact would never change.

The first night Selma moved into her new apartment, Mirza expressed the urge to sleep over. She studied him with her inquisitive eyes for a while until she finally proclaimed that she was okay with that. When time came for them to sleep, Mirza lay next to her in bed, cozying up to her like an abandoned kitty. He inched closer to her until he undressed her and lay on top of her. Selma remained motionless. She entrusted to let him do whatever appropriate at that moment. She didn't feel anything. She lay in bed, her arms spread as if she was about to make invisible snow angels and her eyes glued to the ceiling. Then it was over. Mirza positioned himself back next to her. He'd occasionally reach out to her hand and hold it, and she'd take it out of his hand and hide it. The night turned sleepless. Mirza felt the yearning to tell her stories that he had not shared with many. While he spoke, Selma looked at the ceiling, her eyes not blinking, and listened to the stories of Mirza's transformation from the war.

He told her that he had gone back to Kotorsko a few years earlier. When he set foot on the familiar land again, a lot had changed. The village that was once friendly, where everyone knew each other and the community was like a big family, now had a whole different population structure. All his old neighbors were gone, and some new people had moved into the houses, repairing them and making them their own. When Mirza visited his home, he barely recognized the house. He looked around to see any familiar spots, but even the trees nearby looked overgrown, some having been chopped down, revealing a view of the small stream leading to the big river. What had become of his former home?

He had cried, and thanked goodness that his parents didn't accompany him on the trip. Their hearts would break at the sight.

The home he used to have was no longer. He didn't belong there. He'd promise himself he would never return. He forced himself to call Sarajevo his new home, the city that he had nothing in common with.

WHEN MIRZA FIRST MOVED TO SARAJEVO WITH HIS family at the brink of the war, their survival mode existed on two levels. The main one, surviving the war, consisted of sleeping in the basement every night as the Serbian tanks shelled the streets randomly, without warning.

Hiding in the basement forced them to get to know their new neighbors. Most of them grew up in Sarajevo, making Mirza's family the only refugees from out of town, with a heavy accent and little education. To assimilate, Mirza sought out boys his age who'd take him in and agree to play with him. He'd watch them play soccer on a nearby field and one day he went up to them. He pointed a finger at the field, as if to ask, could I play with all of you? A boy, with red hair and a missing tooth, signaled that he could join up and he instantly became a part of a team. He didn't care if his team won. He didn't mind if most of his teammates were passing the ball sloppily, unable to keep it on their side of the goal or score. None of that mattered. What he cared about the most was that he'd start feeling a belonging in this city that was never his.

But an hour into the game, a sudden explosion blasted in the middle of the field. It came just as Mirza bent down to pick up the ball and the detonation blasted him a few feet, sending him flying in one direction. He landed on his back, his ears deafened. He couldn't move. Through muffled ears, he heard screams, and for a second, he thought he might have been dreaming.

His head seemed a bit heavy, disoriented, dizzying. In the corner of his eye, he saw a grown man running toward them, and he smirked, thinking that he shouldn't interfere with their game. He followed him with his eyes until they stopped at the scene of two boys lying side by side, both with their legs cut down to their knees, looking as if a hungry animal had tried to eat them.

And then he heard a cry for help. *Help! Over here!* Two men came over to him and grabbed him by his legs and arms awkwardly. From this new vantage point, he could see the entire field, parts covered in the blood of the boys' bodies. He was carried to a place they called a hospital—an abandoned store converted into a makeshift emergency room. Its broken windows were replaced with sandbags for protection, and electricity was powered by a generator.

His ears were still somewhat deafened when he arrived home that evening. They would have kept him in the hospital longer if it weren't for ever-changing shifts of wounded soldiers and civilians needing imme- diate care. His injuries were mild—a concussion and slight damage of ear drums. During the war, most patients suffered severe injuries from bullets or shrap- nel. His parents, who watched over him as he lay in bed, cried, occasionally hugging each other as if they had already somehow lost him. Mirza quickly recovered— his injuries were minor relative to many other boys that day—and after a few days he was able to walk outside to the balcony. His mother had screamed, telling him not to go outside, the enemy could see him and kill him this time. But Mirza felt invincible. If he could have survived the field shelling massacre, he could survive anything.

A few days later, his father, now a recent recruit as a soldier, came home and told everyone a story about how a bomb fell into a trench and blasted his friend, rendering him into a thousand little pieces. His father, a man of steel, as Mirza would see him, sat down at the dining table, placed his head in his hands, and wailed.

Sarajevo had not been kind to him. If he could, he would move elsewhere and start his life afresh. Maybe go to college, get a better job, and help out his parents from abroad. But he had no place to go, no opportunities to improve his life. Now that the war was over, the Bosnians were left to their own devices to improve their country and prosper. Besides, now he had another reason to anchor himself to the city: Selma.

Selma cringed when she heard him say this. She turned away from him to signal displeasure. She squinted her eyes and pursed her lips, feeling angst; she wanted to tell him her own stories and explain why their relationship could never be the same again, but the words escaped her. She pulled the bedsheet up to her chin as if to protect her from his candor.

What Mirza didn't tell Selma that night was when the war ended, Mirza's survival instinct diminished, fading away. While during the war, he had thought of himself as an invincible tough guy, he now felt reduced to a coward. He'd get irritated and upset easily, often breaking household items or screaming at his mother or father, cussing them out, telling them they were the worst parents in the world. He was so enraged that the only way he could cope with his actions was by drinking copious amounts of alcohol until he blacked out and forget what had transpired the day before. His behaviors were destructive in that he would drive dangerously fast, often under the influence. Socially, he'd interrogate strangers, question them about their whereabouts during the war, wondering whether they were friend or foe. He'd meet up with girls, sometime women much elder than him, and have mindless, unprotected sex, not worrying about the potential consequences.

The chaos the war had created in his head was now slowly manifesting itself into almost every facet of his life, and he couldn't avoid it. He felt lucky he could find a job in a bar. During and after his shift, he'd spend half his income on his much needed reprieve: alcohol. He'd hope his war demons would drown and disappear. But they'd linger around, and Mirza's rage would grow each and every day.

Mirza held hope that all that could change now that Selma was back in his life. He'd promise himself he would not show that side of him in front of her, for he didn't want to scare her away. He had noticed that she changed profoundly—something had altered her person, but he didn't know what exactly. Ever since they reunited, he tried to get as much information as possible out of her, but she'd would just dodge his questions by shaking her head or waving her arms. "It's nothing really," she would say.

But Mirza had a feeling it was something profound; it had to be since the new Selma was no longer the happy-go-lucky, charming girl he remembered. He saw her now as a young woman ridden with fears and worries; her pale look and skinny body revealed a hint of sickness—what kind, Mirza didn't know, but she looked unwell. He promised himself he wouldn't amplify her fears with his rage. Maybe he could be the positive force to turn their lives around and return them to their beautiful innocence as they were before the war.

That night was the only night Mirza had a chance to unleash his past. It was Selma's resolve to keep her distance.

❦

SELMA'S ALARM CLOCK WOKE HER UP EARLY. SHE SHOOK off the ghosts from her dreams and put on her dress, preparing for the day ahead.

She arrived at the hospital at Kosevo Hill, an old rundown building with brown façade, which was still pierced with holes from bullets and shell shrapnel from during the war. Repairing the walls had never become a priority. When she entered, she found the rooms were dark, the smell a mix of old puke and blood. It was hard for her to believe that only recently, incarcerated bodies were dragged on stretchers through here, to save whatever little precious life was left in them.

The Kosevo hospital in Sarajevo fought battles of their own in their attempts to salvage people who were wounded, sometimes with their arm or leg dangling from their sockets, or a head pierced with an unwanted bullet. The doctors and medical staff, some of them volunteers from the medical college, would run around, exhausted, their eyes drooping down, unable to concentrate, overwhelmed by the enormity of the situation, from the volume of bodies coming in. Caffeine free, as there was no coffee during the war, they'd be running on adrenaline, transferring the bodies from one room to another, from one bed to another, operating together like a serial production line of saving lives. Many of the patients would end up dying in front of their eyes, helpless. Their hearts would stop beating while the mind was still in shock from being subjected to evil, still not ready to depart from the world and without their family members, some of whom knew nothing of this dying, by their side.

The hospital now functioned like it did before the war. The gynecologist was on the second floor, and Selma reluctantly opened the door. The room looked drab and uninviting, and she couldn't wait to get through the appointment so she could head home. The doctor came in, barely looking at Selma, and appearing as if she didn't want to be there. She put the gloves on and turned to her, gave her a stern look and said: "What brings you here today?"

"I think I'm pregnant."

"You do? What makes you think that?" Her demeanor was still stern.

"I missed my last period... or two."

"I see. Do you recall when you last menstruated?"

Selma put her head down as her mind began to unearth the recent memories. When was it? She couldn't recall. Why was this detail important now?

"No," was all she answered.

"That's not helpful." The doctor came up to her and began to examine her, pressing her hand against her abdomen. "Can you at least remember an approximate date?"

"It was still winter, I think, and around the time I last had intercourse."

"So, you do recall the intercourse?"

"Vaguely. I didn't enjoy it. Doesn't happen often."

"Let's go to the ultrasound. We can check it out today." The doctor exited through the side door and gestured for her to follow. They walked through the dark and narrow hallway and arrived in a room that smelled of death.

"Lie down," the doctor instructed. She did so and then the doctor proceeded to put cold gel on her stomach, which she ran over with the ultrasound transducer. She worked in silence. Selma looked at the monitor, but she couldn't read the blurred image. She couldn't tell if a life was hiding there in plain sight. "I see it."

"See what?"

"You're definitely pregnant. You see here?" The doctor pointed at an area of the image where a gray mess was dancing.

"Do you see a leg? And an arm?" The doctor smiled. "Based on this ultrasound image, you are almost four months pregnant."

Selma lurched upwards. Four months. This hit her as the worst surprise. For a second, she lost her breath and all her senses along with it. She breathed deeply trying to relax on the cold hospital bed.

"Do you want to know the baby's gender?"

But Selma, in her newly created complex world,

couldn't answer. She was thinking of only one thing: she could never protect this baby. She closed her eyes, hoping the dizziness would dissipate.

"You're all right?"

She could hear doctor's voice, distanced and muffled, but it was as if the words couldn't travel up to her brain. She felt a strong grip on her arm, causing her to open her eyes. Above her she saw the doctor, looking puzzled.

"I thought I had lost you for a second."

"Doctor." It was now time to tell her. Time to announce the death sentence. "I don't want this baby."

Another few seconds of silence filled the room before the doctor began to nod her head.

"I understand. Times are rough after the war. But I'm afraid it's too late. No one will perform an abortion at this stage. You will need to deliver."

"Doctor, please. I'm pleading with you. I can't have this baby." Now tears were falling down her cheeks, which took her by surprise. She couldn't recall last time she cried. Heaviness upon hearing the news shook her; how could she ever care for this child with a broken relationship with the father or get by financially? What could she do, with limited love and support, to provide this child a beautiful life? It was too much to ponder. "I just can't."

"I'm quite sorry, dear, but it's out of my hands. I wish I could help you. I really do. Do you have someone who can help you? With the baby?" She looked down at Selma's hands, probably checking her fingers for any potential signs of marriage. "Do you have a boyfriend?"

"He's not my boyfriend. I don't want to be with him."

"I get it. But he's the father of your child and you both need to decide how to best raise this child. And you will tell him you're pregnant. And that you are expecting a baby boy. Hopefully that will put a smile on his face." A baby boy. It took her to the time her baby brother was brought home, bundled up in a swaddle, crying at the first sensation of the world. It took her some time to accept him as her brother—and not as her competition—but once she did, she loved him what all her heart. And yet, she was sure she couldn't replicate that feeling, for she wasn't capable or strong enough to keep this baby safe or protected. For one, she had failed to protect her baby brother. She could never trust herself with another child again.

Over the following days and months, Selma schemed the ways to avoid seeing Mirza. Every time he'd get in touch with her and offer to come visit, she'd find a new excuse. *Not feeling well. Busy. About to go to bed. Need to get up early tomorrow.* He called her and left a voice mail message, asking her point blank if there was anything she was hiding from him. *Hiding? No*, she'd reply. *Just need my space.*

She'd occasionally see Spotty and let her in her apartment. She would cozy up to her while she lay down in bed, resting her growing belly. By that point, she could feel the baby's little kicks and day by day, they were getting more powerful, more meaningful. Each time this happened, Selma would grab her belly, as if trying to subdue or stop the movement.

You don't belong in my body.

She couldn't connect to the being inside of her in any way. She thought of it as a strange object, inserted inside her against her own volition or desire. She felt sick to her stomach, not because of the nausea of being pregnant, but because deep inside, she felt guilt, like she was committing a crime by not wanting this child.

Mirza continued to call her, doing anything he could to try to get through to her, but skillfully she avoided him.

One evening, after having walked through the neighborhood straight from work, tired and looking forward to arriving home and putting her head down, she reached her front door only to find Mirza's large stature standing there. Startled by the sight, she jumped and yelped.

"Hello, baby," Mirza said.

Selma couldn't tell whether "baby" was sarcastic or was full of rage and frustration. She couldn't figure out how he'd got inside her building either. The doors were locked at all times, and you needed a key to enter.

"What are you doing here?" she asked.

"Your question is irrelevant right now. Why are you hiding from me?"

She walked up the stairs nervously and he followed her. When she unlocked the apartment and entered, she noticed how close Mirza was behind her, as if he wanted to make sure he wouldn't miss the opportunity to get into her apartment.

"I'm not hiding. I've been busy." She dropped the key on the dining table. "How did you get in?"

"I made a copy of the keys for emergencies."

Selma cringed at this. She shook her head, her eyes wide. Standing before her, Mirza appeared as a big monster. At that moment, she felt she could never trust him again; from now on, she would never give him any slice of her time.

"I think you need to leave now. You're violating my space and privacy."

"Your space and privacy? What about our baby?" He pointed at her stomach, which at that point was difficult to hide. It stuck out from her body, big and benevolent. "I found out you're pregnant. You thought you could hide, didn't you?"

"How dare you."

"How dare I what," he said, raising his voice. "It's my baby, is it not?"

"How dare you make me pregnant. I never asked for this child."

"Whether you asked for it or not, it is yours now. Ours. You better not hide from me again." His voice still sounded loud and alarming. Selma headed to the front door to find peace elsewhere, but he crossed her path and grabbed her arms, facing her head on. "Where do you think you're going? Huh, huh?"

He pushed her toward the bedroom, her feet trying to catch up to his gait.

In a flash, Selma questioned who the person in front of her was. What happened to Mirza? The sweet boy that he once was seemed to have disappeared. The war took him away. Selma knew he'd never be that sweet boy who once upon a time willingly switched playing his favorite game with the neighboring boys to spend time with her and tell her funny stories to intentionally make her laugh. The new, deformed Mirza was no longer interested in making Selma happy or compromising; indeed, he was ridden by rage inside that made him act like an angry rabid animal. What could she do to get him back, to get any of the past back? War is vicious; it takes a lot from you. It can steal your soul.

"Stop it," she pleaded.

"You're not going anywhere." When they neared the bed, he pushed her hard and she landed awkwardly, her body stretched out as if she was capitulating. "The war is over. You need to shake that shit off, you get it." Mirza wasn't entirely sure what Selma needed to shake off, for she never shared what had happened during the war. But he knew something heavy and unforgivable stood between them. His voice sounded demanding, unpleasant, and the words penetrated Selma's ears.

"The war has nothing to do with it."

"The war has everything to do with it," he insisted. "All your weird habits of hiding and mistrusting the world has got to stop. You've become a weirdo. You understand? Where is the Selma I used to know? Where is the sweet girl I enjoyed spending time with? Why can't you shake off your damn nonsense and live a life? Why?" He still screamed, his face reddening like a ripe tomato.

"Because..." She was trying to give him an answer, something that would placate him, but she wasn't sure that anything would satisfy him in this temper.

"Because what?"

"I don't need to explain anything to you. My body is my right. I get to choose what happens this time." Selma took all her inner strength to say this as if, with those words uttered, she was trying to undo her past.

"What's that supposed to mean?" Selma was caught off guard. But Mirza didn't give her a chance to reply. "Do you take your pills every day?"

"Yes." It was a lie. She had become indifferent, complacent, non-committal to anything that served a real purpose. She failed to see a reason in doing anything that could help her move on or advance to a better life. When she lived in the orphanage, a psychologist, whose origin was unknown to the children, came to visit every week and observe the children. The woman didn't speak a word of Bosnian except for *zdravo*, meaning hello, and *kako si*, meaning how are you. The psychologist would sit there, her long hair hanging in front of her face and covering the notebook she'd place on her knee as she slouched in a small chair. She'd sit like that for an hour, taking notes every few minutes, and then excuse herself after the hour-long session concluded. Afterwards, she would go into Enis's office, the director of the orphanage, and spend a considerable amount of time discussing her discoveries.

After a few sessions, Enis came up to Selma and asked her to come to his office. Enis was middle-aged and had come out of the war married, with two children already old enough to be able to walk to their school on their own. His expression looked empathetic, his eyes drooping downward and his lips always forming a smile, making the arcs meet in a funny and interesting way. Enis always had a nice thing to say to whomever crossed his path. His positivity was contagious and he was always cracking a joke or two.

But the world was unpredictable to Selma and she couldn't trust even this seemingly nice person. She wasn't sure if he was going to turn on her, turn into something different, something she'd have to run from. Nervous that she might have done something wrong and was about to be expelled, she feared for the future. She had no place to go if that were the case.

When she arrived at his office, she knocked on the door timidly, even though the door was wide open.

"Come on in, Selma." Enis said. There was a smile behind his voice, and Selma felt at ease. "Sit down."

It was the first time she was ever asked to sit down, making her feel nervous again, unable to comprehend what was happening.

"Nothing to worry about. I wanted to reassure you that all we want here is help you grow. But we're noticing you've gotten more... how should I say this..." He looked to his left and gave it some more thought. He returned his head and continued, "...more shy. Maybe. Reserved. Reserved might be a better word. We notice you don't talk to anyone here. You haven't made any friends, you don't make eye contact... and we're worried. Worried, might be a strong word, of course. Concerned. That's better, concerned. And we want to help."

Selma waited for the punch line. She shrugged slowly,

anticipating a delivery of something that hopefully wouldn't compromise her state of being.

"I feel normal," was all she managed to reply.

"Well, normal is good. That's very good. But we need you ready for when you head out into the world." He lifted his arm and gestured toward the window. "You will turn eighteen soon and then you will be eligible to leave this place. And when you're out in the world, you gotta find a job you like, maybe even take up some courses in college. Because... the world out there isn't always, how should I say... welcoming. To adjust, it may take some time, but you need to be ready."

He pulled a small box from his upper drawer, and Selma peered her head forward, like a turtle daring to come out of its shell.

"Here, I have this for you." He lifted the box to eye level. He appeared to be reading it. "These will help."

"What are they?" Selma was curious.

"They're anxiety pills. They will help you calm down and be more... yourself."

"I am being myself. I don't know what you're saying." She took offense to his comment. Sure, she was different from all the children living in the orphanage, but she didn't mind. She was perfectly content spending time alone in her room, daydreaming about reuniting with her family.

"But being yourself as you are is just a teeny bit strange. Strange that you don't want to make any human connections. Quite frankly, it just seems off. It is the imperative for the human race to make connections. To feel close to one another. To procreate. To feel human. To accept fears together and cope with our inevitable immortality. Are you saying you'd prefer to do this all alone?"

"I'm perfectly fine alone." This conversation was over, as far as Selma was concerned. She didn't appreciate being judged or told she needed to change. They both paused and looked at each other with a long stare, neither blinking.

"Selma, sweetheart. Please do me a favor. Take these pills and see how you feel. I want you to succeed in the outside world. I want you to be happy in life." He extended his arms with the pillbox in his hand. Tentatively, she reached towards him and grabbed it.

"Okay. I'll try."

He smiled. "Great. Please do. Take one a day; that should be enough." Selma dipped her head to disguise her sad eyes. Even the seemingly nicest person ended up judging her. Could she still trust him, she wondered? She turned around and walked out of the office with the box in her hand.

Since that day, she'd take the anxiety pills, yet she still felt the same. They made no noticeable difference, except that they sometimes made her feel hungrier than usual. When she got pregnant, she abandoned them all together.

"Yes, I take them," she repeated. Now that Mirza was interrogating her, her only choice was to lie. She owed him nothing.

"Then what the hell. They don't work. You're weird as hell."

Still on the bed where he'd thrown her, Selma propped herself up, getting on her elbows, with her head up high as if she was about to say something, to deliver a speech even. But she just looked at Mirza, hoping he'd leave her home. She touched her belly ever so lightly and then moved her hand away quickly so as not to give Mirza any impression that the idea of being a mother was growing on her.

"You need to leave. Now," she said, her voice emboldened, which caused Mirza to do a double take, in disbelief. "Now. I decide this time. It is my choice."

He looked at her but had nothing to offer in return. He wasn't entirely sure what Selma was talking about, but he surmised it was about taking the pills. He didn't want to argue any longer. As he left her bedroom, he turned one more time and said, "Your choice. It better be the best one."

He then quickened his pace and walked out the front door, leaving it open. Selma could hear his feet skipping the steps as he ran down, followed by the loud slamming of the door of the main building. She lay back on the bed, sighed and managed a smile: for the world, she was finally ready.

UNITED STATES OF AMERICA

THERE WERE ONLY A FEW DAYS WHERE EMMA COULD recall being truly happy: the day she graduated from college, the day she got married, and the day Dr. Huang called her to confirm she was pregnant.

The IVF procedure was finally and successfully over. The constant needle poking accompanied by taking drugs, and attempting to manage the stress had taken its toll on her, and she now prayed the first cycle would be a success. Her emotions were all over the place as her hormones reacted to this unnatural way of becoming a mother.

All her troubles vanished though when one month her period didn't come, and to validate this miracle, she took a pregnancy test.

She waited in the bathroom for the red line to appear on the stick, indicating her pregnancy was real. When it came, instinctively, she screamed and ran out looking for Michael.

Hearing the scream, Michael freaked out and ran toward her, trying to figure out whatever trouble she had got herself in. But when he saw her waving the stick in one hand, and the other covering her mouth, he then realized. Their dream was coming closer to reality.

In disbelief, she looked down at the stick over and over again just to make sure the line did not transfigure into something else, thus wiping the sign of pregnancy at once.

"Oh my god, oh my god." Emma kept saying, empty of any other words. She snapped a photo of the pregnancy test and sent it to her sister.

Hey, guess who's becoming an aunt soon?

Belinda responded within seconds:

Oh my god! CONGRATS, sweetie! I know how much you want this. Super excited for you! <3

A few days later, the new fact set in: she was going to be a mother. An entirely new human being for whom she was going to be responsible was going to share her world. She was slowly coming to understand that she would have to stop indulging in small things like going out on a whim with her friends, or sleeping in on weekends, or sipping wine at night until she got giddy. All of that needed to be forgotten, at least while the baby was young.

Emma made all the ultrasound appointments in advance, and she wouldn't miss any of them for the world. Michael accompanied her on her first appointment, happily skipping work for the afternoon. At the doctor's office, Michael would hold Emma's hand while Emma lay on the bed and they'd relish the sights of a little life showing up on the monitor. There was no end to their happiness. They'd be all smiles.

When she entered the third month of her pregnancy, she was ready to share the news with everyone and anyone she could think of.

"Honey, let's wait with the announcement. We can throw in a surprise party and invite our family and friends."

"We can still do that. I think my friends *deserve* to know now." She had spent a considerable amount of time texting her friends, informing them of their progress. They'd be supportive, often ending their messages with the words *I'm praying for you*, or *I'm sending you the good vibes*.

She called each of her friends in Chicago and, one by one, they'd scream, causing Emma to hold the phone away from her ear.

"Oh my god," Catherine screeched. "That's wonderful!" In her high-pitched voice, she told Emma how she would love to come to Boston and plan a baby shower.

"Are you moving, too?" Catherine asked.

"Moving?" Emma felt this question as a provocation from Catherine. Her friend knew she and Michael lived in a small space and seemingly didn't approve of their lifestyle. It was as if Catherine expected everyone to live a luxurious life, to jump on a band wagon and get rich and live happily ever after. But she didn't want to succumb to her provocation. "Well, we've been actively looking at houses in the neighborhood, but we haven't come across that perfect house yet. You know how it is." Emma let out a nervous laugh.

Their one-bedroom apartment was nowhere close to being ready for the baby. They'd need to carefully maneuver around the space as it was so cramped. Perhaps they should sell their treadmill to make room for a basinet and they'd eventually need to move the dining table to the corner so the baby had space to play when it was bigger.

But this was all temporary, Emma would remind herself. People lived in smaller spaces and yet were happy. If anything, it would make their familial bond stronger with everyone being in such a small cozy space, in close proximity to each other. A house would eventually come. With the real estate bubble about to burst, an affordable house was just around the corner; she could feel it.

She couldn't compete with Catherine. She married a former hedge fund broker so she was set for life. When she gave birth to her first child, she left her job in a boutique store and turned into a stereotypical stay-at-home mom, ensuring the house was in order and all meals were cooked while at the same time maintaining her looks with her hairdo and nails always being done. This was typical Catherine though, even before she became rich. Even when they were children, Catherine would distinguish herself by wearing pink at all times, with hair bows and sparkling shoes. Emma had always preferred comfort: a pair of loose slacks and a T-shirt.

By the time she married, Catherine had already forgotten what it felt like to be from a middle-class family, constantly worrying about the security of her job, or paying the mortgage on time. Getting nails or hair done became just as important as cooking a meal or raising children.

As much as Emma disliked the differences between her and her friend, she appreciated Catherine's gesture. She'd do anything to move her happiness forward.

The first trimester went splendidly. Emma would eagerly go to all her appointments, where the doctors monitored her closely as if she was a rare precious jewel. She was told her pregnancy was considered high risk, because she was already at that age—thirty-eight—where women's biological clocks began to tick that bit slower. By the second trimester, the small bump on her belly had begun to form, the life that she promised to nurture and love protruding out of her in a way she could see.

At her ultrasound appointments, she'd ogle over the image, marveling at the living blob displayed on the monitor. One of the ultrasound technicians gave her a short tour of the body parts: *this is the heart, this is the head, these are the legs.* The thought of having two hearts inside her made her feel special. She'd downloaded an app to follow the size of her baby grow week by week, from a pepper corn to a blueberry to a strawberry. She'd picture the baby in its full form and finally in her arms wanting nothing but love and the basic necessities to survive.

Emma decided that she wanted to have a gender-reveal party instead of a baby shower, but when she announced this plan to Michael, his immediate reaction was, "How are we going to pay for it? Things are already a little rough money-wise."

"I talked to Catherine. She's organizing it." It wasn't ideal, no, but Emma found another opportunity to show Michael she was in control of the situation. They had options. People in their lives wanted them to succeed and to show their full support.

"Catherine? Your childhood friend Catherine?"

"Yep. She said she'd sponsor the whole thing." In her excitement about the party, Emma ignored the fact that she felt jealous of Catherine at times. Catherine had no reason to worry about money. Ever. Even when she announced Catherine's willingness to pay for it, her voice sounded a bit flat, with no usual excitement that Emma was known for.

"Seriously? You don't even like Catherine, for crying out loud."

"What? When did I say I didn't like her? I never said that."

"You don't need to say it, Emma. You call her a frog

and names like cross-eyed all the time. What's that all about?"

"Oh, I just joke. I've known her forever."

Michael shook his head in disapproval. "None of this feels right to me. First, your parents lend us the money, and now Catherine is paying for the party. What's next? Your boss is gonna buy us a house?"

Emma laughed.

"That's funny. Everyone is just happy for us. Having a baby is a big deal, honey."

"Whatever." Michael shook his head and exited the room. Emma let out a deep sigh, hoping Michael's bad mood would soon pass. She wasn't letting any negativity get in the way of her happiness.

The gender-reveal party came and went, which seemed to have sealed Emma's high spirits. The party was too early in her pregnancy, but Emma grew restless waiting to share her happiness with her friends.

When Emma and Michael arrived home after the party, she slumped down on the couch exhausted. Pregnancy sapped the energy out of her, but attending the party and all the attention completed depleted her.

Michael's brows were furrowed and he seemed as if he was going to smash something. His teeth were clenched and his hand made in a fist. What was he so angry about? Emma felt uneasy.

"What's wrong, honey?" she asked.

There was a long silence, making the air heavy and unwelcome. Between his teeth, Michael finally uttered. "I can't believe you lied to me."

"Lied to you about what?" Emma felt an invisible punch to her stomach. The only thought she associated with the word "lie" was the loan she took out and hid it from Michael, telling him her mother lent them the money. She expected him to be surprised, but not so enraged. She had never seen him this angry before.

"Your mom and I spoke today. When I thanked her for the money, she said she had no idea what I was talking about."

"I can explain." Her words rushed in order to subdue his rage. She had to find a way to calm him down and reassure him things were in control. There was nothing to worry about.

"I was so embarrassed and ashamed. You lied to me. How could you? Why did you? And where exactly did you get the money from if not from your parents?"

Emma lowered her head and bit her lip. The sight of her belly protruding reminded her why she took out a loan then concealed the truth in the first place. In the end, it was worth it. She had achieved her desired goal. She looked up and gave Michael a stare. She finally said:

"I took out a loan." Telling the truth was the only way to go now. Emma was sure that Michael, upon hearing what she had done, would offer a smile, shrug his shoulders, and act as if nothing had happened.

"A loan?"

"Yes. A loan," she said, regaining full confidence. Without the loan, goodness only knew if they would have ever been able to seek out treatment and conceive. It was a wise decision on Emma's part.

"Why couldn't you tell me? I don't understand."

"I didn't want you to worry about it or get discouraged."

"Are you serious? Are you fucking serious, Emma?" His face reddened.

"Keep your voice down."

"You're making a decision about this child like you're the only parent. What about *me*? Where do I fit in this decision-making process? What is this bullshit?"

"I'm so sorry. I really messed up." Emma's guilt surfaced despite acknowledging her well-made decision. Maybe she should have told Michael about the loan earlier, so the air was clear. If she apologized, perhaps Michael's rage would disappear. She needed his understanding and forgiveness. She needed him. But Michael was emotionally out of reach.

"This is my child, too. Don't forget that, god damn it."

With that final word, he grabbed a jacket and stormed out of the apartment.

Emma was shocked. She felt empty, as if someone had grabbed her and shook everything positive inside of her until it disappeared. She couldn't recall ever seeing Michael this angry. Ever. Perhaps the stress was eating away at him, having realized the enormity of becoming a parent. It was a big responsibility and a life-changing event. She reasoned it was different for men—they often obliged in a woman's desire to have children as nothing physiologically internal was driving theirs.

A little after midnight, Emma heard the front door open and close. Michael was making an uncontrollably loud noise in the hallway, making his presence known. Whenever he made a loud commotion at home, she knew he must have gone drinking. Emma knew Michael didn't take alcohol well. When he drank too much, Emma feared he'd become somebody else, that he'd resemble her father perhaps—directionless, lost, lacking self-esteem. She feared that, if Michael continued to drink often, he'd never become the father her child deserved.

She should be asleep now, having been exhausted from the party. But she couldn't close her eyes, and she stared at the ceiling wondering what could transpire from her interaction with Michael. In Emma's mind, one lie couldn't set him off so badly. With their happiness of her getting pregnant abound, Emma would expect Michael to see her point of view and to move on from his anger. She waited for him to come in, lie next to her, hoping he might give her a gentle hug, but Michael was a no-show, a bad sign.

From that moment on, everything began to turn frosty between them, interactions just formalities. There was no more love in their exchanges; he'd ask her how she was feeling, with the absence of a touch, a smile, a caress, and then simply respond to her questions in a politely appropriate manner.

She was now attending the ultrasound appointments on her own. When she saw her baby dancing on the monitor, she'd smile, but this passing happiness often faded as she had no one to share it with aside from the medical staff.

Most nights, Michael would show up at the house around nine or ten in the evening, way past office hours, without any explanation as to where he had been or why he was late. But Emma didn't want to ask or inquire about his strange behaviors. She was afraid whatever Michael shared would shake up her happiness or affect her pregnancy. While she waited for him to arrive home, she'd cozy up on the couch and read a book—she'd go back to the same page and read it twice, for her invading thoughts didn't let her concentrate. Her books were her only companion while Michael was out drinking, and she was starting to feel alone.

Now, she only had her son, the new love of her life.

One Monday morning, at four months pregnant, her stress began to show even more evidently. Michael had already left for work, and the night before, he'd slept on the couch. Sleep deprived, she placed her shoes on, but before she crossed to the door, she noticed she put them on the wrong feet. *What the hell.*

She decided to walk a couple of blocks before she caught her bus. There was a coffee shop on the corner that she wanted to go to first to get a hot brew to help her wake up and be more alert. With each step, her mind went into a strange cycle, putting thoughts into her head that made her sad one minute and happy the next. Her husband was now so distant, like a million miles away, but her son was so close to her now that they were almost one person. She couldn't reconcile this new realm. She needed her husband back. But what would it take for him to forgive her? She needed him, and his forgiveness could help her feel more at peace.

"Emma, if I may say so, you're not looking well right now," Mary said as soon as she saw her. "Do you need anything?"

"Oh, I'm fine. Thank you, though."

"Are you sure? You just... look quite unwell." Mary must have been referring to her pale face, no make-up on, none of her usual spark or grace.

"Yeah, I'm sure. If you don't mind, please close the door behind you when you exit."

"Sure will." Mary sounded cheerful, despite showing a grave concern for Emma.

When she opened up her email, there was one from Derek that drew her attention. Her tired eyes scanned the subject line and noted the exclamation point indicating the urgency. This had to be important.

Emma,

We lost the Rilley Associates over the weekend, after they informed us they were unhappy with our service. Two million dollars down the drain. Let's meet ASAP to give you more details.

I will need to know: How can you fix it? Figure it out by the end of this week.

Derek

Emma wasn't too surprised by this news. After she talked to Thomas Rilley, she stayed in her office until nine in the evening to finish up a folio for the Rilley Associates. But the more analysis she was doing, the less sense it all made to her. She was becoming cross-eyed and the numbers on her computer screen were melting into one giant mass. When she looked at the clock, she was surprised how late it was, especially with so little accomplished. She promised herself she'd get some good night sleep and wake up early in the morning to finish up the task, but the following day, she had trouble with it again. It took her much longer to complete the client's request. When she finally did it, she realized she had missed the deadline. *Make that tomorrow*, Rilley's words echoed. She was in trouble.

Derek's email deeply concerned her—it was the last thing she needed. How could she get back their client? Was there a way to fix things to make the unhappy customer happy again? If she could, she would undo her lie to Michael and fix the awkwardness between them. But all signs showed she was far from reaching that goal.

She stood up to go the bathroom but had to grab on to the desk, for she felt dizzy. She stopped to regain her balance and come to her senses. She stood in the same spot for nearly a minute before she moved forward.

In the bathroom, still dizzy, she felt like she needed to rest, so she sat in a stall for quite some time. When she decided it was time to go back to the office and face the challenge, she stepped out and caught her image in the mirror: she hardly recognized herself. She looked strange and disfigured. Suddenly, the image started to blur and contort, sending her into a different world. Before she could even question what was going on, her body slid down beneath her and hit the ground. She lay for a moment, staring up at the ceiling, the space turning into one large block of color without its borders, shades or shapes. And then suddenly—a blackout.

⚜

WHEN EMMA OPENED HER EYES, SHE SAW HER MOTHER standing next to her bed, her eyes sympathetic and worrisome. Behind her, she could see Michael in the corner of the room, looking stoic and cold. She moved ever so slightly, her gaze dancing between the two of them. When she noticed an IV hooked onto her hand, she realized she was lying in a hospital bed.

But she couldn't speak just yet. She couldn't bring herself to open her mouth and ask what had happened to her, why she was in the hospital.

"Here you are," her mother said, followed by a deep sigh of relief. Emma saw a single tear forming in her mother's eye. Why was she crying? What was she doing here in the hospital?

The whole scene was terrifying. The last thing Emma recalled was being in the bathroom, her image disappearing in the mirror as she felt to the floor.

Michael approached her, watching closely as she oriented herself in the new environment.

"Hi," he said gently.

Emma still couldn't utter a word, just stared at the faces in front of her. Her mother stroked her hair while Michael continued to look at her inquisitively.

It was as if there was nothing to say, so they all waited in silence.

The doctor coming in to check up on her provided a reprieve.

"She just woke up," her mother said, before asking, "Are there any more results? Do we know what's happening to her?"

"Yes, we just got the blood test results. It appears that Emma suffered from a seizure. Was it known that she had epilepsy?"

Both Michael and her mother shook their heads. Epilepsy was new to them. Emma stared up in the ceiling, listening in to the conversation but not adding anything. She was still gathering the energy to simply be.

"We have also examined the baby. The placenta seems to have prematurely separated from the uterus, causing a fetal injury. This is quite typical in pregnant women with epilepsy whose condition is not closely monitored. Seizure episodes are typically exacerbated by exhaustion or a lack of sleep. Unfortunately, the baby did not survive the fall."

Emma continued to stare at the ceiling, unwilling to accept what she had just heard. Her world ended right there and then. She had nothing. Her body was void of soul, and now life, too.

"Are you sure, doctor?" she heard Michael ask. "Can we get a second opinion?"

Emma listened as the doctor said she was quite sure and began to explain the next steps: a surgery later that day to remove the baby from the uterus.

When the doctor exited, like a devil flying from its fire flame, Emma finally found her voice.

"No." she whispered.

"What, darling?" Her mother took her hand and caressed it.

"It can't be true. The baby is still alive. I can feel him moving inside me."

"Oh." Her mother uttered a wail through her tears.

"It's not true. The doctor is lying."

Michael stood up and approached the bed, where he lingered awkwardly, as if he wanted to say something, but the words were escaping him. Before either he or her mother could offer any words of wisdom, Emma repeated, "I know my baby is still alive."

She placed her hand on her belly gently.

"Why don't you get some sleep, sweetheart," Michael said, trying to tame her denial. "Sleep will be good for you."

By the following day, the news had already reached the fertility clinic. Dr. Huang called Michael to find out how Emma was holding up.

"She's okay, at least physically. Emotionally—not sure." He had walked out of Emma's room for privacy, but still whispered the last part. "She thinks the baby is still alive."

"That's quite normal," Dr. Huang replied. "She's in the denial stage. I've talked to her doctor at the hospital and been appraised of her condition."

"I see," Michael said. "What do we do next?"

"She needs to recover. Every woman is different, but

recovery can take anywhere from several days to several months. Knowing Emma and how much she wanted this baby, it could be even more."

"I get it. But once she recovers, what do you recommend we do then, doctor?"

"Do in terms of what?"

"Should we try for another baby?" Then, a brief silence. "Doctor Huang? Are you still there?"

"Yeah, yeah. Of course," Dr. Huang said, though it was clear she was figuring it out what to say. Eventually, she elaborated. "I am not going to tell you what to do with your lives—certainly everything you do is your personal choice—but I will have to share with you that the odds are not in your favor. With Emma's health condition and the amount of stress her body has endured, I would highly recommend that you avoid any future IVF procedures. I'm afraid you'll only be wasting your money and time, and adding unnecessary stress and frustration."

"That... doesn't sound encouraging at all."

"I understand. And I'm sorry. Like I said, you can certainly try again, but your chances of conceiving will be reduced with each cycle. Even if she did get pregnant, the epilepsy would make her pregnancy a lot more challenging."

"What else can we do, Doctor Huang? We want to have a baby." Michael wasn't sure his words rang true to him. In an instance, he realized he was using the words Emma would be choosing. He empathized that Emma wanted a child, but he was no longer sure about it. With the recent turmoil in their relationship, he wondered if having a child was a good idea. Could they return to their happy stage and sustain it? They both suffered and needed time to heal. Now was not the time to deny the difficulty of bringing a child into this world. But he was willing to listen. He was ready to learn about other possible options.

"Your other option is finding a surrogate mother who will deliver for you. But the costs could amount to a very high number—an average of hundred thousand dollars. If you can afford it, it's a great option. And then, of course, there's an adoption…"

But Michael was too focused on the costs. "A hundred thou—" Michael had a hard time getting words out of his mouth. "Did you say a hundred thousand dollars?"

"Yes. Unfortunately, there is nothing more I can do to help you. I certainly wish you and Emma all the luck. And again – I'm sorry for everything you've gone through. In case you do decide to move forward with the IVF, I'm here."

"Okay, thank you, Dr. Huang." Michael managed to say empty words.

The line went silent. Michael still held the phone to his ear as he tried to comprehend the information. A hundred thousand dollars. For one life to begin.

He began to rage. Who puts a price on a life? And the cost didn't even include the day-to-day expenses for the child once born, like daycare, which he knew equaled the cost of their monthly rent, or food or clothes, or toys or books. Michael did the math in his head, and all he could conclude was that his and Emma's dream of having a child was anything but reachable.

After all the events the past month, one thing Michael knew: it was best not to shake Emma's hope. He would keep the surrogate mother option from her. It was his turn to keep a secret.

✣ 6 ✣

BOSNIA AND HERZEGOVINA

KOTORSKO, THE VILLAGE SELMA LIVED IN BEFORE THE war, had a friendly, welcoming society. All the neighbors knew each other by name, by home location, by family structure and characteristics, by values, by habits ingrained from the past generation, and by the amount of fortune each family acquired, thus informing how hard working or clever they were. The final attribute, which seemed less important, was people's religion. When a neighbor uttered someone's name, everyone knew exactly what religious background they came from. If they said their name was Mladenko or Radovan or Aleksandar, this person was most likely an Orthodox Christian, and often equating religion with nationality, Bosnian people mistakenly identified themselves by where supposedly the Orthodox came from: neighboring Serbia. But these people were not Serbs, per se. Nor were they Serbian.

Similarly, a Branko, Tihomir, or Josip living in Bosnia would be called a Croat, though in actuality, they were Roman Catholics.

Then there were Muslims, which were simply just that—Muslims. Not having an "identity" of their own, Serbs always wanted to believe that—and insisted that—Muslims were Turks, and thus should return to Turkey. They had no regard for facts or history. But the truth was that while under the rule of the Ottoman Empire in the sixteenth century, many Slavs that were of another religion converted to Islam so they could avoid paying taxes on their property. Bitter by the takeover of their land and the Ottoman's power to wipe out their large population, Serbs took their frustrations out on the contemporary Muslims, blaming them for what transpired five hundred years ago. According to them, Bosnia should be split right down in the middle; the eastern side returned to Serbia, and the western to Croatia, where they historically belonged. But to Muslims, that'd be like splitting your heart right down the middle and disappearing like a stream of blood.

The centuries-long hatred, which was well concealed during the time Tito ruled, was passed down quietly from generation to generation through odes, poems, and literature. Serb parents would teach their kids to call Muslims *Balija*, a derogatory name, and they'd slaughter pigs in their backyard as a demonstration of how Turks should be killed. Kids, the observant little creatures that they are, would fantasize about such endeavors, and when the Bosnian War arrived in 1992 many ultimately had the chance to put those skills and desires into practice.

Selma knew little about the religions in Bosnia. Aisha often would tell her she needed to marry a Muslim man, of her own kind, so there was no mixing of the blood. It wasn't a hatred speech of any kind. It was a warning, one to protect her from heartbreak, or at least the headache of integrating herself into a new culture: she'd have to cook pork for her husband, which was against Islam. She'd have to listen to a group of men singing Serbian patriotic songs accompanied by a *gusle*, a one-string instrument that sounded like a screeching animal. She'd have to attend church. She'd have to forget about circumcising her son if she ended up having one. She'd be even forced to perhaps wear a cross around her neck. She'd forget who she was or from whence she came.

Her grandmother, when she was still alive, would tell her a story of how mixed marriages played out in a symbolic way in which a Serb male would reach out and invite his *Balija* lady to snuggle up on his arm. To solidify her point, she would shake her head in worry, exhale loudly and say, "I don't trust them. They're all the same."

Her maternal grandmother was a character. Wise beyond her education, which consisted of four years of primary school, she had a special gift for problem-solving, no matter what the problem. She ended up having nine children, three of them dying at young age of illnesses, which were incurable at the time. In the midst of winter, when the last of these children passed away, she was told that the mortuary had no way to bury the dead and that the cemetery was "closed" until the snow thawed out. But her grandmother couldn't stand to watch the deceased child lying on her sofa—cold and pale—for the sight pained her, so she decided to dig a hole in her back yard and temporarily bury the body there until the cemetery resumed its normal function.

With the death of her grandmother, Selma no longer had anyone trying to indoctrinate her with beliefs about the Serbs, Croats, or anyone else for that matter. She was still young, barely a teenager, and she was happy for her days to consist of school, games and cartoons. No longer were these stories, which had always been whispered in households, shared among the neighboring children. In school, she was told the stories of partisans, Tito's soldiers, liberating the lands from the German Nazis or Italian Fascists, and she learned to be Tito's pioneer. Tito was clever: while he commanded, he made sure that history books did not mention that Serb Chetniks, a newly formed paramilitary group from World War II, slaughtered Muslims in Bosnia. Or that the Ustasha, Croatian paramilitary groups, did the same. All Selma heard were heroic stories of the Nazi defeat by Commander Tito—no wonder he was the Yugoslav hero people bowed to and cherished.

When Tito died in 1980, the delicately balanced domino pieces began to fall and everything was regressed back to square one. As soon as his body was lowered into his grave, scheming about a potential ethnic war resumed.

THE BOSNIAN LANDSCAPE WAS MOST GLORIOUS IN THE early autumn days when the leaves began to turn yellow and red, and the fresh scent of grass lingered in the air. Each day, the temperature began to cool by several degrees, and the days were getting shorter, the darkness enclosing the narrow and less visited paths of the village. Summer days, which sometimes returned temporarily, seemed heavy and out of place, as the people of the village were getting ready to hunker down in preparation for the long winter to come.

1992 began as an entirely ordinary year for the Karic family. A year like many previous ones. Selma's mother dutifully prepared sauerkraut in a big barrel, leaving it in the basement so that the heavy stench didn't permeate the rest of the house. She'd also cook pounds upon pounds of eggplant and peppers and then grind them, turning the hot mess into an *ajvar* spread. They'd slaughter their oldest cow out by the barn, cut it into pieces and freeze some of it for the winter.

Now that Aisha had to care for Selma and her brother, Selma watched her turn a bit frantic and pulled into too many directions all at once. She'd often burn food on the stove or forget to take the laundry out of the washer and hang it on the lines. One time, she promised to wait for Selma in front of her school so she could take her grocery shopping after classes—Selma's favorite—but after twenty minutes of waiting, it was clear to Selma that her mother was a no show. It was almost like she'd forget the world existed outside her four walls. While Selma got glimpses of the news about the turmoil in Croatia—sometimes in the newspaper, and sometimes from her classmates—her household seemed void of any discussions on the topic as if they lived in a bubble.

Did her parents simply forget a war was raging in a neighboring country? Did they not care or worry in the slightest?

The war in Croatia was at its height. The bloodshed was being reported in the news on a daily basis. Serbs had occupied a number of cities in the northern and south-western parts of the country where a few towns had been razed to the ground. Thousands and thousands of people were killed and displaced.

With the ordinariness of their daily lives, the Karics never suspected that this war was a precursor to the one to come in Bosnia. They reasoned that the stories Selma's grandmother used to share were old wives' tales, as they were far from anything they had ever previously experienced. They had never had any trouble with their Serbian or Croatian neighbors. The lines were never crossed; the cultures were never disrespected; the mingling and mixing of social circles never caused any angst or confusion. If Aisha wanted to go to the nearby mosque, she could. No one waited for her on the steps to block her way.

They never suspected anything. Except for a few.

Those few had a task at hand. The task was to gather everyone's names in the village and hand them over to the "authority." What type of authority this was, no one knew.

When their Serb neighbor came to the door and asked for the Karics' information—their legal names, date of birth, religion—Aisha stood at the door, with Selma on one side, and Besim resting on her hip. Selma looked at their neighbor with her head down, her big eyes penetrating his. She was noticing how differently their neighbor behaved, and she was perplexed by it. He didn't smile. He didn't ask her mother how everyone in the family was. He didn't ask to come in, and refused to when her mother offered. Selma felt a chill in her bones. Something was off. For the first time ever, she didn't feel safe around her neighbors—the missing smile, and the seeming hatred in his eyes alarmed her. What was he angry about? What had her parents done to him? Were they in trouble?

"What do you need our information for, Mladen?" her mother asked in a quiet voice. Selma could feel her fear.

"Just a simple survey."

"You need to know about our religion?"

"That's what I was instructed. To get your religion."

"But you know we are Muslims, Mladen, though we don't go to the mosque often. We didn't even sacrifice a lamb for Eid this year."

"I hear you. It's just a simple survey. Nothing to fear." Selma felt tension in the air; she observed Mladen's mean eyes resting on her mother as if he was about to harm her. Her mother's face remained troubled, but she forced a smile to subdue the tension. Despite Mladen's reassurance, fear was palpable.

"I don't feel comfortable giving our information, neighbor. No one should care if we go to the mosque or not. Selma hasn't been to a mosque in ages."

He looked at her with the same unsmiling eyes then back at her mother. He raised his arms overhead to show his impatience.

"Listen, I don't make these decisions. I'm here to get what they need."

"Who's *they*?" Her mother's agitation was beginning to show. "What's someone going to do with our information?"

"I don't know. I'm just doing what I'm told to do." He jotted something down in his notebook while the three of them stood there and waited for the interaction to end. Besim began to cry loudly and Aisha began to hush him, fearing his sudden outburst might introduce more awkwardness to the situation. Mladen snapped off the pen he was holding to close it and slammed his notebook shut. "All right, neighbor. I have what I need. Take care."

With that, he turned around and rushed through the front yard to the next house.

⊙⚇⊙

THEN CAME THE WINTER. THE BOSNIAN HILLS WERE gently covered in the white of snow, which effortlessly melted into the hazy sky. Following the most recent news about trouble brewing in the country, the families in the village were all locked in. The politicians were arguing about the fate of Bosnia, whether it would yield to Yugoslavia or stay loyal to its already broken borders. Slovenia and Croatia had already made themselves independent, and the Bosnian politicians hinted that their country might go down the same route, but the resistance among the Serbian contingent was obvious.

"We won't let that happen. Bosnia belongs to Yugoslavia," one argued, with the intent that Yugoslavia would then turn into Greater Serbia, a plan designed long ago.

Selma didn't understand any of this turmoil. The angry look in her neighbor's eyes stayed with her and she would shudder whenever she thought about it.

Despite the tension in the air, everything else seemed to be normal. No other signs of trouble ensued. Selma would come home to a cooked meal every day. Often, the sweet scent of cinnamon would welcome her; her mother would usually make a *kompot* with the apples from their backyard, mixed with sugar and cinnamon. The fire in the large baking oven would crackle and heat the house with its enormous and powerful flames. She didn't think of it as anything unusual, just something she'd needed to appreciate. Not every child had this privilege. Her mother, not having worked in a job a day in her life, was a domestic woman who only cared to make sure her family was well fed, warm, and happy.

When she returned home from school each day, the first thing she would do was pick up Besim from the crib and give him a big kiss on the cheek. By then, Besim's eyes were solidifying into their blue color; his cheeks were getting prominent and bigger; his thighs enormous. He'd coo to his big sister, occasionally attempting a smile. His alertness was growing each day, like a flower slowly opening up and spreading its scent. Besim was a beautiful baby, and Selma would hold him, hug him so tight that once she felt him gasping for air before beginning to cry.

Selma often caught her mother looking at her and Besim longingly, and smile. She once told Selma her two stars finally completed her universe and she felt whole.

At times, her mother would go out of the house to get more chopped wood and coal for the stove. Selma would follow her mother with her eyes through the window and watch her cross a small path to the barn, walking carefully so as not to fall on the sheet of ice. This was her daily task. The stove constantly demanded a lot of fuel to feed the fire. Only occasionally, she'd see a neighbor from a distance and she'd wave.

A few days after the neighbor's visit, Selma heard her mother outside: "Mladen, ooooh, Mladen," she yelled out, her feet locked to the ground. She was shivering from the cold of her light outfit, patiently awaiting a wave back. But one never came. Mladen seemingly ignored her. In fact, he did not even look in her direction before he disappeared behind the nearby hill. Aisha stood there, taken aback by what just transpired. He probably didn't hear her. She was cold, so maybe her voice was muffled from her shivering mouth. Or maybe he was rushing somewhere.

No matter. She proceeded to walk to the barn to get the wood.

When she came in, Selma was holding Besim while he slept soundly, occasionally moving his head left to right, right to left. Aisha put the wood next to the stove and came to sit down next to her.

"Mom?" For the first time ever, she noticed a fear in her daughter's eyes that she had not seen before.

"What is it, darling?" Fear spread within her like the fire in the stove.

"Is there going to be a war?"

"War? Why would you say that? Where did you hear?"

"Some kids in the school say war is coming. Is it true?"

"Oh, don't listen to those kids. Kids say all kinds of things."

"But... Dragan stopped by the school today and came up to me, he seemed so angry I thought he was going to beat me up. I didn't do anything to him to anger him. He then told me Muslims were pigs and we should be killed because we are bad." Selma watched her mother's eyes fill with horror. Aisha shook her head slightly while Selma was waiting for her mother to give a reasonable answer. There had to be a good reason Dragan was saying these terrible things.

"Oh, dear. Dragan is a mean boy. Don't listen to him."

Selma had heard her mother describe Dragan as a mean boy many times. It was this moment that her mother had a chance to listen, to evaluate what her daughter had to say. Killed? Like pigs? How could a child utter such harsh words? Kids didn't have such wild imaginations to project such ugliness, intimidation, hatred. Even mean boys didn't have an imagination this wild to think of a bloody, senseless massacre. No, they would have heard it somewhere. From their parents, most likely. She thought back to her earlier encounter with Mladen. Should that not raise red flags, jump-start her into the high alert mode?

That evening, Aisha shared what she heard Selma tell her with her husband. He stopped in his tracks, pausing for a few seconds then turned around.

"Dragan was always a troubled kid, wasn't he?"

"I guess."

But they both pushed the darkest thoughts away; they had to. There was no way war would come to their beautiful peaceful village. They'd shudder to think that their house would be shelled down or occupied by an enemy, or, worse yet, that they would be taken away, all remnants of their lives disappearing into the darkness.

The winter passed peacefully, with snow falling vengefully and cutting off the roads to Doboj. But the Karic family was safe in their abode, having enough food for the harsh cold winter days.

When the spring came, and the snow began to melt, making small puddles in the yard, they grew alarmed. When they watched the news on TV, they'd see the army and tanks freely roaming through the streets of Sarajevo as if they had just aided in liberating the city. They'd sit on their hard couch and watch the buildings go up in flames. Out of one tank peeked a head with a hard helmet on, a young soldier showing his face. They were horrified by the conspicuous smile he held—was it him who was shooting at the Sarajevo citizens?

The airport was flooded by confused looking folks who seemed to be catching the last wave of flights that would take them away from this newly created uncertainty.

But Selma's parents didn't know what to make of all this. They were still convinced that this was only temporary. That it was a mistake and all would go back to normal.

They went on with their lives, spending their days watching the sun breaking the horizon and turning the snow into water. They'd put their children to bed, snuggle them up in warm blankets and give them a big kiss good night. They'd go to bed early, while the fire was still flickering in the stove. For winter days, even mature ones, were boring, uneventful, and sleep was the best option.

When spring came, the uncertainty had turned into chaos. The news was now filled with stories of the Yugoslav Army taking positions on the hills and mountains surrounding the capital. Her parents would shake their heads in dismay, wondering who could be a mastermind of such anarchy. For them, war was for the riches, and therefore far-fetched for their world. They were just peasants, somewhat invincible in their perceived insignificance. All they wanted to do was live a peaceful and happy family life.

They pushed away any dark thoughts, of any possibility of the war coming to them. Their only mission in life was to love and protect their children.

⚜

MARCH HAD PROGRESSED THE WINTER TO ITS END, AND almost all the snow had thawed and melted. Mornings were still cold and raw, keeping people inside until late morning. Battles were raging all over the country, where Serbs who had arrived freshly from Serbia and Monte Negro, began their raging storm of ethnic cleansing. The Muslims' only curse was their name and that they had been born into a Muslim family.

The Serbs attacked the capital and besieged it in a matter of hours. They began turning Bosnian villages into their own, enriching themselves with the possessions and properties that once used to belong to Muslims.

Selma went to school one day only to be told to go home. Lectures were canceled for the day. Mirza looked at her with relief in his eyes; he hated school and would rather play with his friends in the forest.

The following day, they'd shown up again, and again were told to return home—and not to bother coming the following day. The school was closed indefinitely. Rumors were going around the village that a Serbian paramilitary group was coming, but Selma's parents didn't pay them any heed.

"What nonsense. Even if they come, we didn't do

anything. What are they going to do to us?" her father had said.

When Selma went to Mirza's house that evening, the house seemed eerily empty. The front light was off. The usual busy-ness inside a house that one could usually sense from outside, even when the lights were out, was absent. Where was Mirza and his family? As she looked through the windows searching for any proof of life, all she found was darkness and emptiness. Why wouldn't Mirza tell her anything? Where would they have disappeared to? It all seemed suspicious—Mirza told her everything and never kept a secret. She walked home slowly, head and shoulders down.

In the morning, Selma was asleep, snuggled up in multiple blankets to stave off the cold, when a strange commotion in the house suddenly woke her up. A few minutes earlier, in the midst of sleep, she thought she had heard screams outside, but she wasn't entirely sure whether it was part of her dream, so she turned around and kept sleeping. But as the sound became louder and more intense, she slowly peeled her eyelids open until she was fully awake. The sounds were coming from the kitchen and the living room.

The clock on the dresser showed five thirty in bright red neon lights. It was quite unusual for her parents to be so loud at this time; regardless of the season, they'd get up around six thirty, ignite the flickering fire in the stove and make coffee.

As she dragged her sleepy body downstairs, it was the smell that she noticed first: gunpowder, alcohol, and heavy body odor, all mixed in one sniff. When she entered the kitchen, she found two men she had never seen before laughing and opening the kitchen cabinets, searching for something. One turned around and was taken aback when he noticed Selma standing at the door.

"Look who we have here," he yelled.

The other man turned around. They both had long beards and a hat with the *kokarda*, a sign of Serbian paramilitary group, chetniks. A gun hung on one of men's shoulders. Another gun was sitting on the kitchen table. The man who had yelled, when he smiled, revealed rotting teeth with too many cavities, the upper tooth four missing from his right side.

When she turned to run away, one of the men grabbed her by her hair, which was still messy from her restless sleep.

"Hey, where do you think you're going?" His spit was flying through his clenched teeth.

"Who are you?" she asked quietly, in her naiveté. "Where are my parents?"

"Your parents? Your parents are gone, vanished. *Balijas* don't belong here no more."

She could hear Besim begin to cry in the other room, and they all paused. Now that Selma heard his sweet voice, fear kicked in. She felt as if she had transported to another universe, another dimension, one that was no longer familiar or safe, now void of her parents, or the familiar morning pattern of snuggling up to her mother while she was sipping coffee or talking to her father. Even though only a few minutes passed since she realized their disappearance, it already felt like she'd been missing them for a whole eternity. She wanted to cry and scream, but the fear clenched her body, preventing her from feeling anything else.

Her baby brother. If her parents were gone, to goodness knew where, how could she run away with her brother? She had promised, the day of his circumcision, she'd protect him forever and keep him safe.

"That's my baby brother."

"Oh, your baby brother, you say." One of the men said. "I will take care of the baby brother, Dusan, and you take care of her."

The man with bad teeth walked out of the kitchen, following the crying sound, while the other approached her and grabbed her arm, pulling her to the kitchen table.

"Lie down!" he screamed.

Selma positioned herself on the kitchen table, belly first, next to man's gun. Her right cheek was facing the stove, and she could feel the heat coming from it. She could also feel the weight of the man behind her, slowing putting pressure on her body, becoming heavier and heavier. She could barely breathe. His face was now near hers, and she could smell the heavy stench of alcohol, mixed with perversion and evil.

She could hear her brother's cries getting closer and she tried to jerk from the man's fist to catch a glimpse of him.

The following instant, she felt the man's hands move downwards, and he lowered her pajamas to her knees. One hand moved quickly, grabbing her between her legs.

He pushed his fingers inside her so hard that it stopped her from having any other sensation in her body. She winced, but dare not say a word, for she was so terrified. He removed his hand temporarily and began to unbuckle his belt.

Besim's cries was now in the kitchen, yelling with an enormity and power Selma had never heard before.

She felt the man push inside her. She wasn't entirely sure what it was at first, but after some time she realized it was his phallus.

But she had no time to even process what has happened, for out of the corner of her eyes, she could see something much more horrific. The other man opened up the stove, revealing the fire flaming wildly, and placed something inside, placed her *baby brother* inside.

The sound of his cries began to dwindle slowly until they came to a complete stop, disappearing only into her memory.

She clenched her teeth. A single tear rolled down her cheek. Physical pain wasn't what she was feeling any longer. She felt her soul leaving her body. She had nothing. The only thing she had at this point was void and emptiness.

When the man finished with her, he got up, finally lifting his weight from her body. A heaviness fell upon the room, and all Selma could hear was the sound of his belt buckling, and the flames of the fire in the background.

The man then grabbed his gun and walked away with

the other man to investigate around the house, to see if anyone else was there.

"You go down to the basement, I'll go upstairs."

As if someone had extended their hand to her, Selma pulled herself up and slowly stood on her bare feet. She looked down and saw blood on her lower pajamas. She looked at the stove one last time and then headed toward the front door.

She found herself in their front yard, which was covered in snow-melted puddles. She felt the cold beneath her feet, as she stood on small patches of snow. She looked to the right, and to the left, looking for traces of her parents, but there was nothing. Her feet were starting to feel numb and before they could give out, she started to run.

Ahead of her was the main path into the city; on the side of her house was a forest that led to a place she hoped was out of harm's way. Maybe she'd run into her parents, walking hand in hand, smiling at her, telling her she should have worn her boots. They were probably safe somewhere, wondering what their kids were up to. As she ran, she'd mistake the trees for her parents. She'd pause to touch them, to feel them, but all she could feel was the rough bark of a pine tree. She kept running, occasionally turning around in case her parents were chasing her, turning the chase into a hide-and-seek game. In her mind, they'd all stop in the middle of the forest and laugh loudly, and her parents would tell her that she had woken up from a bad dream.

She kept running, looking for a safe place to stop and

find comfort. Her parents would be around the corner –
no doubt—and her mother would tell her to put her
boots on and go wake up Besim in the crib.

She kept running and hearing her baby boy cry,
cry, cry.

She kept running until her feet gave in and she fell to
the ground, her body awkwardly spreading out in the
snow. The clouds above began to spin and spin around
until a veil of whiteness moved her to a different plane.
And then, everything turned dark.

⊗≀⊗

SELMA WOKE UP UNDER A BLANKET, ITS SMELL
unfamiliar to her. She felt a tight embrace that she
thought was her mother's, but when she looked up, she
was startled by the sight of an old woman in all black.
The woman smiled at her and brought her closer, grip-
ping her tighter.

"You're not my mom. Where's my mom?" she yelped.

When the old woman smiled, she could see her
yellow dentures which had leftover food stuck in them.
The odor from her mouth made Selma nearly puke. But
she was more concerned about where she was.

"Where's my mom?" She repeated and began to free
herself from the tight embrace, pushing the blanket away,
but she had little to no strength to move. "And who are
you?"

"Little darling, we found you lying in the field close to
our house. You're safe, don't worry."

Relieved she was no longer in danger, Selma's desire to see and touch her mother only grew stronger.

"I want to see my mom. Where is she? Where is my dad?"

The old woman looked at her, not saying a word. Her smile turned into a grimace. She didn't quite know what to tell her.

"I don't know where your parents are," she said eventually. "But you're here, safe with me."

Selma began to cry, hyperventilating, gasping for air. Her life seemed to have turned upside down in a heartbeat. She no longer knew where she was, what had happened to her family, who the two bearded men were and why they did what they did to her and her baby brother. She wondered whether life was worth living anymore. She would never see Besim ever again, never kiss his cheek or listen to him coo as she hugged him. She had promised herself she would protect him. She had failed.

Then she learned the hard truth: a war was raging in every corner of the country. Ethnic cleansing wasn't just a hint in the news; it was a harsh reality. The war might have taken her parents away, eaten them alive.

A few days later, she was resting in bed, still in the old woman's house. She tried to collect herself and find her bearings. The old woman was a Serbian woman who lived in a village next to Kotorsko. She lived alone. Her name was Radmila, Selma later found out from the papers she found on the kitchen table.

Radmila had lost her husband a couple of decades

earlier —she found him lying helplessly between the corn bushes, holding his chest. She'd screamed out for help, but their son was too far to hear her. By the time she reached the house, her husband had already died, his eyes tranquil, looking up at the sky. Ever since, she'd worn black. A black skirt and a shirt with a vest over it, and a black scarf. It was the way Orthodox women showed their internal grief. Selma knew this. She wondered why Radmila never remarried.

When she was able to get up, Selma approached a small bedroom off the main hallway and looked at herself in the mirror. When she lifted her head, she noticed she had a long cut sitting across her neck. She couldn't recall when or how this cut appeared. It was entirely possible that the bearded man cut her, tried to kill her as if she were a pig. Strangely, the physical scar did not hurt.

Rape. It was a long time before Selma learned that this was what had happened to her, what that word even meant. Those tough and ugly Serbian men used rape as a weapon as did many others during the Bosnian War. They considered themselves brave Serbian soldiers, even though, in reality, they were only small-time crooks, emboldened by the chaos to act like raging beasts. They belonged to a paramilitary group, because their hatred for others and desire to kill anyone who didn't share their mold were too difficult to tame. As a pack of wolves, they'd march to the known territories where they had planned more carnage. They'd kill, torture, and rape.

Rape.

Selma was a chosen target, easy in selection, for there

she had no defense. These men knew what they were doing. They consciously decided to penetrate not just into the physical part of her body, but also into her soul, knowing their act would ruin it forever. Their weapon would forever mark her as damaged, leaving gaping holes, emptiness. Some of their victims would bear unwanted children whose mixed blood would never flow freely and clearly ever again.

Shame on those men.

They knew that with the permanent damage of their soul, women would walk in eternal fear, resenting the fate they had been handed, hating the fact they could never undo what had been done onto them, realizing their body was just an object that was there to express irrational anger and hatred.

Shame on those men.

Most sadly, these men walked freely, as soon as they pulled up their pants. They would find a new victim, then a new one again. They used their evil weapon unequivocally as if it was their calling. They'd most likely forget their victims quickly, as soon as they walked away even. They'd forget their name—if they ever knew it—their eye color, their shape and size, whether their hair was pulled up or let down, their voices and cries. They'd forget everything about the women they raped. Because, they didn't matter. All that mattered to them was the power they wielded.

Shame on those men.

Would they ever repent? Confess their sins? Or did their Orthodox God not care?

❧❦❧

AS THE DAYS MOVED ON, SELMA'S CURIOSITY ABOUT Radmila grew stronger and she wanted to learn more her. From what she could visibly tell, she lived within quite modest means; her house consisted of only a kitchen, two small bedrooms, and a bathroom. Radmila didn't seem to eat much, but she always had freshly baked bread at home. When the smell of baking wafted through the air, it would remind Selma of home and her mother's cooking. She'd hide in the bathroom and let the tears push away her pain. Selma wanted the answers to her never-ending questions about their whereabouts, but the major question remained: were they even still alive?

The war was raging in Bosnia, with fates similar to Selma's occurring in many homes. But as long as Selma stayed with Radmila, she was safe. They now lived in a predominantly Serbian territory and the war barely reached this part of the neighborhood. She was physically safe.

When Serbian soldiers came to visit, Radmila wouldn't hide Selma. They respected the old woman. And because Selma was already scarred and marked as damaged, no further action was needed in their eyes. When they came, Selma would keep her head down, not looking any of them in the eye. Radmila would offer them fresh bread with butter and a shot of *rakija*. They'd laugh and get giddy and after a feast, they would continue on with their journey.

At first, Selma didn't want to speak with Radmila at

all. They'd sit in the same room across from each other, Radmila would look at her and smile and Selma would shoot angry looks in return.

But one day, after the soldiers left the house, and the two were once again alone, Radmila whispered to her, as if she was telling her a little secret no one should know.

"You'll always be safe here." She winked a couple of times and smiled. "If you want to know the truth, I don't support this war."

Selma looked up to see Radmila's face turn grim and sad. She had a feeling Radmila wanted to convey that not all Serbs were the same. Not all enemies coming from the same group were like those men. A lot of those who succumbed to the politicians' propaganda had issues of their own. They were not grounded in reality. They either were too attached to their identity—and had to fight its superiority or defend it—or didn't know their identity in the first place and had to latch onto the politicians' false words. Those who didn't succumb knew what the world was all about. They had a wider vision of life. They knew life wasn't worth fighting a war—rich or poor, cultured or not—because life was about accepting the ordinariness of it and simply waiting for the mortal stage to end. War wasn't about winning or losing. It was about obtaining control and reaping its benefits by inserting one's perceived authority. There was no such a thing as victory. Both sides lost. There was no way to escape from your own mortality.

"I recently lost my son in a battle," she continued. A couple of tears began to roll down her face. "A few days before I found you. My only son. Before the war started, I told him not to bother joining the army, but he was determined. I told him wars were dirty and pointless. He didn't listen to me."

She grabbed a handkerchief and blew her nose. Silence filled the room for a minute or two until Radmila composed herself.

"Why didn't he listen? He listened to his friends instead who told him he should fight for our ideals. I tried to tell him politicians have dirty and evil minds. They don't mean well for us commoners. But he didn't listen. My son lost his life, because a politician lost his mind. Losing a child, my dear, is one of the most painful pains. I don't know if I will ever come to peace with it."

She brought her hand up to her face to dry a tear and then lowered her head.

When Selma heard Radmila's story, her sorrow, and her pain, she began to feel her stomach tighten and palms sweat. She felt sorry for the old woman.

But surprisingly, Radmila's face then brightened again and she exclaimed: "I'm glad I found you, though! You'll be safe as long as I live. I don't believe in this war, but I have to pretend I do."

Selma didn't say anything. Radmila's relief to have found her didn't match her own.

As the days went on, Selma was hanging by a thread, clinging on to the hope that her parents were somewhere safe, alive, and looking for her. She was dreaming of the moment when they would be together again as a family. In her mind, she saw her baby brother running on the fields between the pumpkin patches behind their house, laughing and extending his arms up to reach the sky. She wasn't quite sure that what she saw was a reality. It was quite possible she was dreaming. The morning was still young and, in her somberness, she couldn't tell dreams from reality. But in her mind, it was possible that her parents had walked away with her baby brother, and they were all somewhere safe. The fire burning in the stove might have been a log—perhaps the soldiers wanted warmth while they rummaged through the cabinets.

She didn't want to know the truth. She'd rather live in denial, for it was too painful to fathom her brother's horrific passing.

A year into the war, the status quo was still as it had been that day. The war seemed to have spread around the whole country, and lives were lost in ever increasing amounts.

Three years passed, and Selma and Radmila continued to share the same space. Neither one talked much. They minded their business, just trying to survive the war and their losses.

But sometime in November of 1995, word spread that the war was concluding. There was no longer uncertainty as to what would happen next, what would be destroyed or who would be killed. The only certain thing was that the war devastated and ravaged the land and its people.

On a December day, at dusk, Selma stole out of bed. The sun barely showed on the horizon and the stars in the clear sky were giving light to the bare land. Making sure Radmila couldn't hear her, she slipped out and walked through the forest, hoping not to run into anyone. The cold morning made her more alert than usual, but it did not stop the sweat from clamming up her palms. She was noticing the small houses in the near distance. She had not seen these during the war.

She kept walking, with steps large and determined that would perhaps lead her to finding her parents alive and waiting for her all along, until she landed on a familiar field, the neighborhood she grew up in. She hadn't realized how close her home was to Radmila's. The entire time she had lived there, home had been only a walk away.

But now, appearing grand yet deserted, the house sat like an abandoned domino block, covered in fire soot, doorless, windowless, and void of life.

She closed her eyes and counted to ten. She was hoping that the silence and pause would remove this scene from reality, but when she opened her eyes again, the ruined domino still stood there. Only then she felt the anxiety go up her spine. She wanted to cry, but she couldn't. She couldn't cry, because the shock of seeing her old home left her without a breath, her mouth agape, and her eyes wide open.

What happened to her home?

She approached the house and walked through the entrance, which was now open and airy. The place smelled of fire and soot. Inside, she found nothing and nobody. It was empty yet still full, for the memories therein were flooding her mind.

She recalled her parents sitting in a corner of the living room and smiling at her. Her mother would cook a meal on the wood stove and occasionally get up to stir the pot. Her father would often read the newspapers of the day, though he always liked to pore over the ads as opposed to reading the actual news. Her baby brother was placed on the couch in the living room so he could be close to their mother when he woke up hungry or wet.

Selma walked to her room, which she also found empty. It appeared that everything had been taken by the enemy, including her parents. The stove was also taken, and with it, the ashes of her beloved Besim. She'd hoped that at least she could get a hold of what remained of him, but that, too, was long lost. Deep down, she had hoped he was still alive, but the second she entered the house, she recalled the morning the soldiers infiltrated her home, her life, and her body.

But what had become of her parents and where they were still remained an unknown. A mystery she hoped to solve.

Selma went back to Radmila's, feeling spent and exhausted. That day she couldn't eat at all. She didn't speak to Radmila, not a word.

The new image of her home—destroyed to the bone, cold, and empty—lingered on her mind. She had not realized how close the destruction was to Radmila's home. The proximity to her destroyed home pained her, made her feel sick to her stomach. For this reason, she resolved to get away from it. She couldn't escape from the memory of seeing her home in newly created fashion, but she could find a place where reminders of it would become sparse.

Two days later, early in the morning, Selma left the warmth of her bed and prepared to leave this place that had become her home. She had heard there was an orphanage opening on the outskirts of Sarajevo. Still a teenager and now most likely an orphan herself, she was eligible to live there.

Outside, she turned around one more time to see where she had spent her war days. In her mind, she thanked Radmila for her generosity and hospitality, then continued on the familiar path, heading toward Doboj where she planned to catch a bus to Sarajevo. As she walked fast, not turning back once, she promised herself never to return. She'd leave her heart and soul here in the hopes that they'd reunite with her family someday.

❧ 7 ❧

During the Bosnian War (1992-1995), an estimated
hundred thousand people were killed; around two million
people were displaced; and fifty thousand women were
brutally raped.
... fifty thousand women were brutally raped...
... women were brutally raped...
... brutally raped...
... **raped**...

❧ 8 ❧

UNITED STATES OF AMERICA

THE SECOND EMMA LEARNED SHE LOST HER BABY, SHE couldn't bring herself to eat, sleep or do anything she'd usually find pleasure in before the loss. Her body was turning into a skeleton; her soul seemed to have departed her along with the baby. The hospital kept her for a few days after the surgery, with the nurses bringing her food three times a day, which went untouched. The nearby table was full of flowers her friends and family sent to cheer her up, but they, too, went unnoticed.

She'd stare at the same spot on the wall, as if she were concentrating on finding a new meaning to her life. At those moments, the most raw, when she was reminded of losing her baby, Emma wanted to die. The spot on the wall became her only companion.

Her mother left the day after, because, as a teacher, she couldn't afford to be away for too long, but Michael came to visit her every day. There were no interactions between the two of them, though, for Emma appeared like a statue, a sad display of a woman who lost her precious one. He'd hold her hand in the hopes she'd react or finally say something, but for Emma, it was as though he were a passing thing in her veiled world.

"Emma darling," he'd say, his voice soft and comforting. But Emma wouldn't acknowledge his presence.

The nurses would come in and out often, checking up on her. After a while, they gave up offering her food, since they knew it would be followed by another rejection. It was clear to all that Emma had fallen into deep depression. Her world seemed like a bad dream she'd never come out of. The dream had no ending or exit—indeed, she was trapped in a waking nightmare.

"Emma, darling." Michael tried again. "Should I bring you pretzels and carrot cake, your favorite?"

Nothing.

"Please tell me what you want or need. I'm here for you."

No thoughts or ideas comforted her. She had lost her baby boy forever, and it was time to deal with the cold harsh truth. In her darkest moments, her thoughts shifted to the past. Her guilt would try to come up with stories on how she could have prevented the death of her baby boy. What could have she done differently to preserve the little life inside her?

She didn't want Michael to visit her anymore. She would watch his shadow on the wall dance back and forth, back and forth, and she was getting tired of the constant commotion in the room.

"Don't come tomorrow," she finally said after many days.

Michael, who had been fidgeting until she spoke up, suddenly stopped. He was happy to hear her voice, which suddenly sounded deep and raspy, even if it wasn't the words he wanted to hear. She had finally said something, after all this time.

"Emma!" He raised his head to take a look at her, a smile forming on his face. "I'll oblige, but you will be released from the hospital in a couple of days. I will have to pick you up then."

Without looking at him, Emma said, "Okay."

It didn't matter where Emma was at any moment. Whatever physical space she occupied felt tight and uncomfortable. She'd rather be nowhere.

Michael was at a loss. When he arrived home, he wanted to hide every single trace of their preparations for the baby. He couldn't protect her from the grief, but he could try to protect her from the further pain of constant reminders. They'd already gotten a bassinet, which they'd placed in the corner of their bedroom. Zero size diapers were in the closet. Bottles and pacifiers were in a kitchen cabinet for easy reach. The baby shampoo was on the bathtub, next to the baby tub. He'd have to come up with a plan on where to move these, for their apartment was so small, unsuited for storage. But they had a small space in the basement, which Michael decided to clear out for this purpose.

As he was looking through the drawers of the dresser for something for Emma to wear when she left the hospital, he spotted Emma's doll, which was looking up at him dully. He tipped it upside down so he didn't have to look at its ugly face. He'd move the doll back tomorrow, before Emma came home. In the drawer, he also found a piece of paper, folded in two. It looked as if it came from a diary. He unfolded it and recognized Emma's familiar handwriting, beautiful and cursive.

On the piece of paper was a poem.

Waiting

I waited for your smiles

I waited for your cheeks

I waited for your soft skin

I waited for your arms.

I waited for your joy

and I waited for your love

I waited for my joy

Flying like a dove.

The wait was worthwhile.

Now you are here,

In my arms

My son.

He let a long sigh out, folded the piece of paper, and put it in the back pocket of his jeans.

Two days later, Michael returned to the hospital to pick up Emma. She walked slowly, her head down, with her unkempt and dirty hair covering her face, with eyes deeply etched into their sockets. Gone was the luscious, bright woman Michael had first met. Now devoid of any kind of joyful expression, gesture, or even feelings, Emma looked like an unknown creature, like a depraved monster from a horror movie.

The doctor handed him a couple of documents, one of which seemed to be a note for Emma's workplace to release her on medical leave. The doctor had predicted she would need at least a month to recuperate from the surgery and the impact of the baby loss. But for Emma, her recovery would need a whole life-time. She could never move on from this experience. The doctor also prescribed psychotherapy to help her learn to cope with her loss.

When they exited the building, the bright sun blinded Emma's eyes. She squinted, hoping she'd be soon out of its sight. People around her looked like plastic figures, moving forward like marionettes on strings. She no longer had personal attachments to people. She felt empty, disconnected, half-alive.

When they arrived home, she headed for bed immediately. She buried her head in the pillow, trying to ignore the sounds from outside, the cars on the street and the bustle on the sidewalk. She'd heard Michael moving around in the kitchen, running water in the bathroom sink, typing on his computer—every single sound was compounded and seemed loud and obnoxious, like big, heavy drums beating in her ears. He would occasionally enter the bedroom to check up on her, to ask her if she needed anything, but she would always shake her head without looking in his direction. All she needed was peace.

DAYS WERE CARBON-COPIES OF EACH OTHER WHEN Emma spent her time in bed all alone. She had lost a sense of time and she couldn't tell how many days had passed since her medical leave or what day of the week it was. Most of her calls remained ignored; she'd occasionally respond to her mother's texts informing her she was indeed still alive and doing okay to keep her worries at bay. The calls dwindled over time, bringing Emma a sense of relief. She'd occasionally look out the window and notice the days getting longer. Spring was around the corner, promising more smiles on Bostonians' faces, now that the harsh cold and snow was behind them once again.

One night, Emma woke up to a loud bang of the front door. Like in a bad dream, she sat up, startled and afraid that someone might be breaking in. Being physically weak, there was no way she could defend herself against the intruder. She almost forgot that Michael was at home, in the living room and he would probably be the first line of attack. Before her mind ran wild, the bedroom door opened and Michael's shadow projected on the wall. His stance was a bit wobbly; Emma could smell alcohol and then she realized he was out drinking again until late at night.

"Michael?" She whispered.

"What the hell do you want, Emma?" He was barely annunciating his words and he elongated the "m" in her name.

"Michael, were you out drinking?" Emma pulled the cover closer to her face as if to protect herself.

"Shut up! Why the hell do you care?" He was making steps toward the bed. He took his jacket off and threw it to the floor. Emma felt her heart beating out of her chest.

"I care, Michael."

"You should care about yourself. Look at you. You haven't gotten out of bed for days, like some kind of a loser." He was now standing near the bed, his shadow wobbling on the wall.

"Michael. Please. Don't."

"You don't!" He approached her and yanked the bed covers out of her hand. She felt the cold air hitting her face and torso. She shivered. "Why the hell don't you get up and face the world, eh? You can't live like this for the rest of your life. If you want a husband, you should pull yourself together and be presentable, damn it."

Emma didn't say a word. She felt a tear wet her face; her stomach tightening with grief. She had been exhausted and her road to recovery was difficult. Whether it was the sudden waking up or Michael's intoxicated words, she had a hard time processing all this. This was the new side of Michael she was discovering. She didn't like it. At all.

"Well, say something!" He raised his voice. Emma flinched. Silence ensued. There was nothing to say. The drunk Michael stood above the bed for a few more minutes while Emma lay in bed, looking up the ceiling, lost for words. She was wide awake, wondering if this was the first distraught night of many more to come. When an alarm outside in distance broke the silence in the room, Michael said. "Fine, be that way. I'm outta here."

He zig-zagged to the door and slammed it behind him.

The night was sleepless for Emma. Too many upsetting thoughts occupied her mind. The scene she just witnessed with Michael was too much to bear. One lie was all it took to get here. How was this possible? For better or for worse? In sickness or in health? It all sounded like a fairy tale now.

In the morning, when the sun peaked through the window curtains, Emma woke up groggy. The scene with Michael from the night before made her wonder if it had been indeed a bad dream. She realized the scene was all but real when she noticed Michael's jacket lying on the floor. She gingerly walked to the living room, stood near the door and looked around, afraid that Michael was still there and was ready to strike again. The empty apartment revealed Michael was already gone for work. She walked back to the bedroom to see if he might have texted or called her, but there were no notifications on her phone. No acknowledgement of the last night or apology?

She curled up in bed and fell asleep.

If before the scene Emma found little interest in anything at all, now she was completely void of any feelings at all. Even the constant thinking she experienced slowly dissipated and she felt like a vegetable co-existing with the space around her. Her staring at one spot in the ceiling was getting old, so she'd close her eyes and feel nothing. Emptiness felt comforting.

Emma made herself the prisoner of her bedroom walls. And that was perfectly allright with her.

An indescribable hunger had eventually forced her leave the confines of her bed, so every once in a while, she'd come to the kitchen and reach for the cabinets to grab snacks. She'd also go to the bathroom, of course, only to see her face in the mirror transformed into an unusual form. She barely recognized herself. As she stared at the gaunt image to get to know it better all over again, she realized she disliked it.

After a month of this, Emma decided she couldn't continue like this any longer. She yearned to be the old Emma, to live again, to feel the beauty and pain, and to be connected to other humans. Her best choice was to seek help in the form of therapy.

Her therapist's office was located in a building that resembled a two-family house. Emma stopped in front of the entrance to examine it, and, as she looked at the yellow and blue flowers protruding from the flower beds on the window sills, she felt a new sense of meaning in life. She had almost forgotten how much she loved looking at the flowers and guessing what they were or what it took to keep them fresh and alive.

She entered the building and slowly walked to the doctor's office. She climbed the stairs with heavy steps, a sign she had not moved much for the best part of a month. Upon entering the second floor, ahead of her stood the door with a sign:

Amy Aves
Psychotherapist

She looked to her right and noticed a small table and a couple of chairs that served as the waiting area. She looked down at her phone and saw that she had only a minute to spare until the session began. She was about to knock on the door, but the it opened just as her hand was mid-air.

"Hi. You must be Emma? I heard you coming up the stairs," the woman on the other side of the door said.

"Yes, it's me." Emma said, unsurely. Was this a good idea? She wasn't sure who she was or what she wanted any longer.

"Come on in. My name is Amy. Nice to meet you."

Instead of reciprocating, Emma looked around the room. Two chairs were placed across from each other while a small table sat in the corner. A candle in the corner was lit, giving out a fresh and comforting scent of lavender.

"Sit down." Amy extended her arm and pointed it to one of the chairs. When they sat across from each other, Emma couldn't help but notice framed photos on the table of small children. She formed a slight, quick smile before she realized where and why she was here.

"Before we begin our session, I just wanted to go over the health insurance information."

Here we go again. No conversation could go on without a mention of money. After Amy diligently went over her rates, she then resumed.

"So, please tell me what brings you here?" It was only then that Emma noticed the blueness of Amy's eyes. They looked caring with the calm hue exuding curiosity and care.

"I... I..." Even though Emma couldn't utter the dreadful words just yet, she felt comfortable sitting across her new therapist and just be. "I lost my baby recently."

Amy's brows furrowed. "Oh, I am so sorry to hear about your loss."

They let another silence occur, this time for each to absorb Emma's words. This was the first time she had verbalized her loss, or made it known to a stranger. Since the baby passed, she had not spoken with anyone except for the occasional text with her mom. Her home was the only sanctuary and she preferred to remain alone between her four walls.

"Thank you," Emma managed to muster. Her words sounded shallow.

"How did you lose your baby?"

"A miscarriage. At four months."

"Oh, I am so very sorry, Emma. That can't be easy. I'll be happy to talk things out with you and see what this loss means to you."

"Well, it means... it means I'm a failure." Emma dipped her head so she could hide her tears. Amy reached for a box of tissues, pulled one out, and handed it to her.

"I understand how you might feel that way, but it is really not your fault."

Silence.

"Tell me about your husband," Amy said, scanning Emma's fingers, her eyes landing on her wedding ring.

"What about my husband?"

"Have you felt his support during this period of grief?"

"I... He's been different lately."

"And why is that?"

"I... I don't know."

Silence again.

"Do you feel that he has been a good support system for you?"

"Maybe. I don't know." Emma was too afraid her therapist would intervene to extreme if she found out Michael was recently belligerent. The last fight would remain a secret, she decided.

"How would you describe your relationship with your husband?"

In that instant, a flood of memories came over Emma, not only the recent fight. She recalled the sleepless nights Michael's lack of forgiveness had caused her. She was exhausted all the time because of him. She thought about his sudden changes in behavior during her pregnancy, how he was unable to move on from her white lies.

And then it hit her: he was partially to blame for her loss. He caused her an incredible amount of stress, and stress led to her miscarriage. All the sleepless nights, all the worries he imposed on her when he'd come home late drunk and not acknowledge her presence; the life inside her. As if she'd just woken up from a dream, her face brightened from this realization.

"My relationship with my husband... I guess it's complicated."

"How so?"

"He... I lied to him about something. He caught me in a lie and then he couldn't forgive me."

"I see. And how did that make you feel, the fact that he couldn't forgive you?"

"Lonely. Confused." She looked into the distance, almost reliving the experience over again. She tried to take it apart and analyze it. "Betrayed."

"Betrayed. Do you think lying to your husband might have led him to feel the same?" Emma deeply sighed. She regretted lying to Michael if that was what caused the rift in their marriage. But there was no purpose of thinking about regrets now.

"Maybe," she admitted, but then the reasons why she did it came back to her. "I tried not to worry him about the money. He was concerned about how we'd pay for the IVF. I took out a loan without telling him."

"And he interpreted that as you going behind his back to make a major decision about your family?"

Emma felt her heart beat quicken. "I... I didn't mean it that way. I just wanted to be in control of our situation."

"I understand. It sounds like your husband got quite hurt by your gesture."

Silence.

"It sounds like you both need some grieving and healing time."

Out of the corner of her eye, Emma noticed her phone, which was sitting on the seat next to her, light up. A message. The name that came across the screen was one she wasn't excited to see: Derek.

What does he want now?

At that moment, Emma realized her medical leave was expiring and it was time to return to work. Her life was seemingly going back to normal even though she still couldn't accept the turmoil that had led to it becoming this way.

❦

THE FOLLOWING DAY, NOT QUITE READY YET, EMMA was choosing clothes for her first day back to work. As she combed through the rack, she realized that everything might look big on her now. She eventually chose a pair of slacks and a blouse that might well conceal her new, skinny figure.

She wasn't getting ready for work because the grief had subsided—far from it; it was permanently attached to her soul—but because she knew she had to get back to the corporate ladder she was forced to climb, no matter how much she now despised it.

The moment she entered the building, everything felt different. The walls looked gray, she noticed. Was that new? She couldn't tell. A ZZ plant was in one of the corners, beautiful and bright green. That, too, was an item she had never noticed before. But it was the colleagues she passed in the entrance who confirmed the change: they looked at her with both sympathetic and suspicious eyes all at once. She gripped her purse tightly, wanting to storm out of the building, but she had to face another demon.

"Hello, ma'am, may I help you?" The man at the front desk greeted her.

"I work here."

"Oh, you do? I haven't seen you before."

"Well, I was... I was away for a while. This is my first day back. You must be new?"

"Yes. In fact, I started last Monday. My name is John."

"Cool." She managed a smile despite discomfort this place caused.

"May I see your badge please?"

"My badge?" Before the receptionist had a chance to respond, she realized what he meant. "Oh yes, of course."

She looked through the purse frantically, almost as if the badge were a safety net. Something, anything that would give her strength to continue and ease the day.

She pulled it out and showed it to John. He made a grimace when he saw the badge, looked up at Emma, and questioned, "This is you?"

She knew what he meant. The beautiful brunette in the picture couldn't compare to the sad, skinny, lifeless person in front of his eyes.

They were interrupted by a voice behind.

"Is that Emma?" She recognized Derek's familiar

tone. She turned around and when he saw her, he reacted as if he had just seen a ghost. "Oh, hi."

"Hello, Derek. It's nice to see you."

"Indeed. Welcome back." He didn't look her in the eye. "I hope we can catch up today. I'm free most of the morning. Just pop into my office."

"Sure." She suspected she had lost her status at work and couldn't get it back. The image of the hard-working, diligent Emma was no longer. But she chose to make peace with it, for she couldn't carry another burden on her shoulders after losing her son.

He continued walking down the hallway, shaking his head slightly.

When Emma arrived in her office, it looked emptier than she remembered it. Did they remove some of her personal items? The "Congratulations" banner on the wall was no longer there. That might have been the only difference, but it spoke volumes. She sat at her desk, and wiggled the chair before sitting on it as if to ensure it was safe. As she waited for her computer to boot up, she watched as people busily walked by her office, none bothering to stop in and say hello.

When she logged on, she noticed how little substance her emails had. Most of them seemed like junk.

Cake in the kitchen

Office birthdays

Would you like to go on a cruise on us?

Staffing updates—promotions and departures

While she dealt with her world falling apart, their mundane life had continued.

She closed her email and resolved herself to face Derek immediately. She stood up and took bold steps to his office. She was glad she didn't run into any of her colleagues and as she reached his office, she knocked on his door gently. He raised his head and told her to come in.

"Hi. Have a seat."

She recalled the day he invited her to his office when he was about to hand her the big promotion. She recalled how complimentary he was that day, pleased with her record history, her performance, and her good standing with the company. She had played her cards well; she had listened to her mentors on how to navigate the corporate world. But now, she had nothing to show for it, and all she felt was that either she had failed the corporate world, or it had failed her. Or it could easily be mutual.

While less proud of her most recent performance, she felt bolder and wiser. She began: "I'm glad to be back, even though I am not in the same condition as I was before my leave."

"I understand." He looked down, avoiding her eyes. "We were quite worried about you."

"Thank you."

"I'm very sorry for your loss. I know how it feels. My wife had a miscarriage before Kayla was born."

At this, Emma jumped in her seat, surprised. Derek had never revealed anything private about himself in the past. She could now imagine a softness about him that he inevitably had, but hid in the cut-throat world of business.

"I'm sorry to hear that," she said.

"It's been a while, but we still feel the pain. Sometimes we wonder what would have become of the little one that never made it." He was beginning to choke up, but then seemed to pull himself together, returning back to his usual, professional self. "But anyway, I have some news that I hate to share. After losing the Rilley Associates last month, the board of directors decided to put Nelson in your place."

Derek paused, waiting to get Emma's reaction, but she barely even blinked. Her face remained unmoved and stoic. No loss could compare to the one she had just endured.

"I know what you have been through, and I tried to explain it to them, but they couldn't get past the Rilley fiasco. You and Nelson will overlap this week to ensure a smooth transition. I'd expect you to be available in case he has any questions about your portfolio. He has been familiarizing himself with the work while he covered for you when you were on your medical leave, so I suspect some of his questions might have been answered already. You will be getting Nelson's portfolio to make the transition a bit easier."

"Sure."

"Starting next week, you will assume your old position. And, naturally, your salary will also revert back to the old one. Nothing I could do there either."

"I certainly appreciate you trying." Emma offered a quick smile. "Is that all?"

When Emma arrived home, she found Michael

sitting on the couch in the living room. She had a double take, as she expected him to be at work. Surprised, she exclaimed, "Hi."

"Hi, Emma." His eyes looked soft, like the times they had just begun to date.

"What are you doing at home?" She looked puzzled.

"I came home earlier to come talk to you. Mind sitting down?" Michael continued with the voice that sounded inviting and serene. He pointed at the couch and Emma looked at it, squinting her eyes -- was there perhaps a trick to his request? She waited a few seconds to ensure Michael was genuine, that he wasn't tricking her into something unacceptable.

"Okay." She sat on a dining room chair instead. "What is it?"

He began immediately as if he had been rehearsing his speech all day long and was now well-prepared for delivery. "I have something important to tell you, Emma, you need to know. First, I want to say I'm sorry about the night I came into the bedroom. I don't know what came over me. I had too much to drink, but that's no excuse, I get it." He paused to see if Emma had anything to say in response, but Emma said nothing.

"There's something else, more important I need to tell you. I've been waiting until you felt better." Emma raised a brow. Did he really think, because she was back at work, she was feeling better? How strange that some people equated the outside world with the inner one. "When you were in the hospital, I talked to Dr. Huang."

Silence.

"She recommended that we don't proceed with the IVF again."

Emma's eyes widened, "What?"

"Given your conditions, she said it would be a waste of our time and money." Michael paused as if he gave Emma space to absorb the information. "And most importantly, I wanted to tell you I've given a lot of thought about having kids. I'm not sure I want to have them anymore." His eyes sloped down at the corners. He choked up, but no tears came from his eyes.

"Well..." Emma was lost for words. She held onto the dining table, for she was feeling dizzy. Michael's image was dancing in circles, becoming slow and blurry.

"I'm so sorry, Emma." He made no mention of the surrogate mother or adoption options, but it wouldn't have made no difference to Emma. He'd better let Emma spread her wings and decide on her own.

She slowly got up from the chair and walked to the bedroom. She lay in bed and buried her face in the pillow to muffle her weeping. She didn't see any of this coming. The reality seemed to have been camouflaged by her absence from the world and her denial of what had happened. Things were slowly coming together. With all the information Michael just shared, Emma's world became a lot heavier and darker.

❦

SPRING FINALLY ARRIVED, MARKING NEW BEGINNINGS. The lush grass and blooming trees on the Boston

Esplanade again became an attraction to frequent joggers and walkers. With the new truth revealed, Emma knew she had to carve a new beginning for herself. Michael was no longer interested in being the father or her child, if she could ever have one. Since he broke the news, living together turned into a formality. She'd hear the front door shut almost every night while she spent time in the bedroom. At least he was kind enough to let her claim the bed indefinitely. Emma hated the status quo and she knew she had to do something about it. More than ever, she was grateful for having Amy in her life, who would listen to her and reinforce or reject her ideas. She was looking forward to the next session with Amy.

And that day finally came. Emma walked a bit faster than she usually would down Mass Ave to avoid the heavy foot traffic and the loud noises that made her cringe. When she turned onto the side street that would take her to her therapist's office, she could hear the sounds of birds chirping and calling each other on the nearby trees. The sounds of nature comforted her and made her realize how much she missed being outside. When she arrived, she noticed the little flowers on the windowsills had sprouted further, opening up their petals, extending their beauty for the passersby. These new sounds and sights gave her hope that healing could happen after all.

She walked up the stairs boldly, as if to make her determination to feel better known. Just as she arrived, once again, Amy opened the door and greeted her.

"It's really difficult not to hear people walk up," she laughed. "Come on in."

Emma sat down on the same chair as last time. She liked the routine. It was as if it was specifically marked for her.

"It's good to see you again," Amy said.

"Indeed. Same here." The words weren't just niceties. Emma really meant it this time. Amy was her only confidant who helped pave her path to healing.

"How are you feeling today?"

"Good. Or, a little better, I should say." Emma felt proud of the words she shared with her therapist. For a long time, she thought she would never leave her house again or attempt to live on with hope.

"That's great to hear." Amy's voice pitched high. She seemed genuine to hear Emma's progress to recovery.

"I've been doing a lot of thinking lately." Emma was looking forward to this moment—the moment where she could finally share all her inner thoughts and feelings that lingered for a while. In her lonely state, she could no longer trust her own thoughts to guide her down a sound path. She'd welcome Amy's feedback to ensure she didn't lose it completely.

"You have?"

"Yes. I know I can't have my son back. I wanted to be a mother so badly. I couldn't wait to hold my son in my arms. Sometimes I try to picture what he'd look like. But that only brings more pain."

"Yes, I can see why," Amy offered.

"But... I had a lot of time to think things through. I

realized I need to get away from Michael and start things over."

"Oh." Amy sounded surprised. "Why is that?"

"He told me the other day that he didn't know if he wanted to have kids anymore. I don't know if I want to stick around long enough to find out if that's how he really feels."

"I'm sorry to hear this. Any idea as to why he changed his mind?"

Emma winced as if she didn't expect this question from Amy. She didn't even consider it until she heard it just now. When the news from Michael hit her, nothing else came to mind to overshadow or question the new reality. "I'm not sure. But ultimately, I don't know if it matters."

"Why is that? Maybe it's just a phase and he'll come around. All this can't be easy on him either."

"That's true. But I had time to reflect on more than just his revelation. I can't be with someone who can't forgive, who will hold grudges for the rest of our lives. He put me through a lot of stress during my pregnancy. All the sleepless nights I spent because his ego and pride couldn't let go. It is almost as if he didn't care about our baby. He was barely ever present when I was being repeatedly stabbed by needles to prepare for my pregnancy."

"Did you tell him how you felt at the time?"

"I wanted to, but I was too focused on my pregnancy. That's really all I cared about."

"I see. Is there anything you want your husband to do to make things better?"

"Absolutely nothing. I thought I knew him well. But I guess I don't."

"Have you communicated all this with your husband?"

"Not yet." Her voice began to crack and she let out a tear she'd been trying to hold in. Amy kept a watchful eye, letting her unleash the pain. After Emma composed herself, she continued.

"Another thing he told me was that Dr. Huang said I can no longer get pregnant. If we tried again, it'd be a complete waste of time and money."

Amy tilted her head in sympathy. "What does that mean to you?"

"It means... I cannot be a mother. I'm a broken woman."

"I see how you might feel that, but a woman is not defined through motherhood alone. We're all somewhat broken, but you still have a choice."

"A choice. What choice do I have?" Emma spoke through her tears, clinging to Amy's words as if she had all the answers.

"Have you considered adopting?" Like the sun breaking through a cloud, Emma's face brightened.

"You know. I just might," Emma said and formed a huge smile.

❧ 9 ❧

BOSNIA AND HERZEGOVINA

"HOW ARE YOU FEELING?" ONE OF SELMA'S COLLEAGUES asked, filing her nails as they waited for customers to show up.

"Fine," she said.

"Do you know what it is?" By now, Selma's belly was large, unable to hide it from anyone any longer. But she wasn't much interested in the conversation.

"I do. It's a baby," the other laughed.

"She's so quirky," the first said after she'd disappeared behind the shelves.

Selma despised the small-mindedness of these women. If she could, she'd hide away from everyone. Since the incident with Mirza, Selma would avoid as many people as she could. She had a baby inside her, yet she felt all alone. Even Spotty came around less often— she must have found better places where food was aplenty and where less danger lurked.

Every once in a while, she'd wonder what her baby would be like: would he end up being tall and heavy like Mirza? Would he have a chin dimple like her father did? Would he have blue eyes like her mother's, ones that you'd just want to stare into and long to be around all the time? She wondered how she would create happiness for him, the one thing she could ensure. It was now her responsibility to provide him a good life, now that his birth was assured. But maybe any possibility of a good life was far-fetched, as far as Selma was concerned. Could she simply hand him to Mirza and his family to care for him? She didn't trust him any longer; the sneaky monster that she now saw in Mirza would perhaps demonize her and say all wrong and nasty things about her when the baby grew up. He would never find out the truth.

At home, she tried to distract herself with watching cartoons, but all of her thoughts turned to fantasies, where she'd see herself sitting on the floor holding her son while both laughed at Tom chasing Jerry, or La Linea making a path until he dropped into the abyss. She'd hold that baby like once she had held her baby brother, and squeeze him tight so he could feel all the love of the world inside her.

But her thoughts would switch like the seasons, and the next moment she'd suddenly picture her son floating helpless in a bathtub, or lying on the floor choking on food until he had a seizure until finally taking his last breath. Selma would picture herself and what she would do in that situation. Instead of jumping to her feet to grab the baby and doing something to help him—perhaps call an ambulance or a nearby neighbor, or take the baby to a place safe, a place that could save his life—she'd just stand there, helpless, with her mouth agape. Her eyes would be wide open, emphatic, but impotent, with her world crushing around her all again.

All human life begins in pain. Their first discomfort starts with their lungs catching air and having to learn to live in such a rush, right there on the spot. It must be shocking to be born, suddenly removed from the womb's warmth. Why else would the little one cry? But that's just the beginning. Every stage, every year, every phase in life represents some sort of adjustment and adaptation to new circumstances. And with it comes suffering. If life was all about suffering, what was the point of procreation?

She'd shoulder these thoughts and continue doing what she knew best: falling into a deep sleep and patronizing with the ghosts in her dreams. Perhaps, there was a better world for this baby where a family would accept it with its open arms; where happiness was aplenty; where a multitude of toys were lying around; where hugs and kisses were a constant gift. Her baby would never feel any of that unless she had a good and caring husband, a clean past and parents who could help her care for the child—not to mention a good job with a decent income. Her baby would never grow up knowing innocence and joy. Maybe someday he would be loved. Not till a better world.

Now that Selma's belly had grown, her sleep was more uncomfortable. She'd toss and turn, toss and turn, until she found a favorable position. The baby would kick in a strangest manner, as if seeking his mother's love and approval. The days were getting longer and warmer, and the summer beckoned. It made no difference to Selma, since she made herself a prisoner of her home regardless of the day or season or year.

One night, as she went to bed, a message from Mirza showed on her phone:

Hey, how are you? According to my math, a few more days, and we're parents. Call me.

Selma just shook her head and pushed the phone to the side.

The following day, when she finished her shift at work, she had a suspicious feeling that Mirza was going to be waiting for her at the door again. Whenever she failed to respond to his texts within a couple of days, he'd show up to investigate, sometimes interrogate her.

When she arrived home, Mirza was not there. But something else was: she found a strange piece of paper slipped under her front door. She bent down to pick it up, feeling the full weight of her belly and having to grab the door so she wouldn't fall. She picked up the note and turned it around.

It's important you come to the orphanage as soon as possible. I have some news to share. Enis.

Selma couldn't even guess what the news was. How she should feel, she had no idea, since she had no preconceived idea of the type of news that awaited her. She could only guess what it might be: they wanted to take her baby away as soon as she delivered it. But, how could they know she was pregnant unless someone had intentionally paid a visit to break the news? Had perhaps something happened to somebody at the orphanage, and she'd been summoned to be told the news in person, as opposed to via text or phone call. The most disastrous of all would be the news that the city had decided it was time for her to return the apartment, for she didn't belong there anymore.

Her emotions were running wild. Her speculation even wilder. She wasn't sure if she should feel elated, forewarned, or cautious. Whatever she was about to hear could tip her emotional equilibrium—hopefully, it would bring her joy rather than sadness.

The following morning, she hushed down her thoughts and got ready to visit Enis at the orphanage. She'd walk this time, she decided. The distance wasn't terribly far, and it would give her some time to clear her mind. She was large and heavy, her feet were beginning to swell, but she made determined steps toward the lonesome building on the hill.

As she approached the orphanage, her heart began to race. She stopped for a second to catch a breath and played with her hair to distract herself. With both hands, she grabbed some long strands and began to spin them around like a rope. It had been quite a long time since she saw a hairstylist. With her minimal wages, she didn't think it was ever a priority.

She opened the gate and entered the ever-so familiar front yard. The roses on the side were trying to spread blooms, but looked more like they were giving up. She noticed that the pine tree, her favorite, was no longer there and she wondered what reason the orphanage had for this sacrifice. She stood there and examined the spot where it had once proudly stood before a male voice startled her.

"Look at you." Enis was standing at the front door with his arms wide open. "I didn't know you were expecting."

"Good morning," Selma offered in return. In her head, she eliminated the option about Enis being sick. What was it he wanted to share? Her curiosity only grew.

"Come on in." He extended his hand as if to aid Selma in her walk, but she paid him no attention. "When is the baby due? He? She?"

"He. Soon," she said starkly, still nervous about the reason for her being there.

"Congratulations. That's wonderful news. If you ever need anything, do let me know. We're here to help."

"I found your note. Whoever left it there." She cut to the chase.

"Yes. Yes. I wanted to share some very important news. Please sit down." Selma stood motionless, slightly annoyed at his request. "Please. This is important."

Selma sat down at the familiar chair behind his desk, and then he followed suit, perching on his chair on the other side.

"I admit I'm not the best at delivering news. Of any kind." He paused, biting his lip. "But you need to know that your parents have been found."

Selma jumped from her chair in surprise and, as if

expecting to see them hiding in the room somewhere—as if they were waiting as a surprise and wanted this moment to be special and fun—started looking around the room.

"So, where are they? Why are they not here?" She stared at him, suddenly hoping that this wasn't some kind of bad joke.

Then a long silent pause. Enis kept his eyes down, occasionally looking up at her only to see her facial expressions change with each glance—surprise to anger to bewilderment.

"Are you going to tell me?"

Ever since she moved to the orphanage, while the other children playfully interacted with each other, Selma would have her eyes peeled on the door. In her mind, her parents were coming to get her. In their reunion, they'd hug each other for a long, long time, in a tight embrace. Her parents would be so delighted to see her grown up and mature. She had started having her dad's features—her eyes and hair were getting darker, and the one cheek dimple pronounced, now more so as she smiled upon seeing her parents after so many years. Then they'd all leave the big city, the city of smog, and go back home where they belonged. Selma would stare and stare at the door, and each time the door opened, a glimmer of hope would rise. But over and over again, her renewed disappointment would awaken as she realized her mother wasn't crossing the threshold.

She had longed for her mother's hugs. Since arriving at the orphanage, she had not received any physical affection of any kind from anyone. She had forgotten what it felt like to be held in someone's arms, close and lovingly. As time went on, she pushed those desires away, for it seemed easier to curtail disappointment that way.

Where were their parents? She had not stopped thinking about them, hoping they'd appear someday. In her heart, she knew they'd never abandoned her.

"Selma. They were found in a mass grave," Enis said, bringing her back to the present.

"What? What do you mean? What are they doing there?" In that moment, she could not fathom the type of things he would tell her.

To explain a genocide would be difficult for anyone to hear. But to explain it to a person whose parents were victims was a task impossible to finesse in any profound way. When the news got delivered to that unfortunate person, there would always be a mixed bag of emotions: anything from sadness to relief to acceptance to rage. But most of all, emptiness. The question, *why me, why my family, what is a life worth with such a cruel act of disposing it* would often cross their minds. But the answer would rarely fill the void.

"Their bodies were excavated with a number of others. It's believed they were murdered at the beginning of the war and buried in that spot. No one knows who exactly did it, but an overwhelming number of people think that..."

Selma tuned out. Her head had begun to spin and spin and spin until she could hear nothing. She stood there, staring at Enis, not blinking.

"Take me home." She said. She wasn't sure she heard all of it correctly but her stomach felt tight. Her dizziness led her to grab the chair so as not to fall down.

Enis stood and rushed over to her, grabbing her under her arm. He led her through the door, then the main gate. They approached his car and he opened the passenger door, so he could help her into the seat gently. He didn't need to ask her where she lived or in which direction. The orphanage had the names of all the parentless, loveless children whose wings they had let fly.

The ride was filled with silence. Selma stared in front of her, looking as if she was not registering anything about her surroundings. When they arrived in front of her building, she opened the door and exited the car without saying a word. She walked as if she were in a dream, yet she was fully awake.

"Selma..." Enis reached out as if wanting to bring her back. He had forgotten to mention that a burial service had been planned for the near future and that she could attend if she chose to do so. He failed to mention that the only way they could locate her parents was through the DNA testing. Technology had advanced to locate the dead, but not far enough to prevent it.

That day had turned into her worst nightmare. Her parents were gone. She tried not to think of the fear and grief they must have experienced at their last breaths.

That night, she had a dream about her mother. Aisha was sitting on the corner of the sofa and she smiled, looking at Selma. She extended her arms, and whispered, "Come, come, my child." As Selma approached, her mother's face became distorted, melting down onto her torso and eventually disappearing into her body. Her smile disappeared with the melting head, and Selma rushed to her. But it was too late—all she could find was a pile of clothes left in disarray.

⚜

WAKING UP THE FOLLOWING MORNING FELT GUILTY and raw. Selma's world had changed before her eyes in a blur of unfortunate news. Unexpectedly. If she could only have one more snuggle with her mother, then her world would be complete. She would let go of her eternally. If she could reach out for dad's arms once more, and be picked up and swirled around. If she could only pick up her little baby brother and kiss his plump cheeks. The absence of these possibilities made her unsettled. She would never see her family again.

It was time to say the last farewell.

But her day turned out to be quite ordinary, as any other. There was no one to grieve with, no one to share her sorrows, no one to lean her head on. Mirza, the seemingly closest person in her life, was ousted in her mind.

She dressed for work and headed out on the familiar path. Everything looked so bleak and dull. The people she passed were mere silhouettes turned into ghosts from her dreams. Blinded by the void in her soul, she walked ahead, not feeling the pregnancy aches, not smelling the flower blooms, not feeling the rain drops, her feet barely touching the asphalt.

When she arrived at the store, she passed by the cash register, not paying attention to the ladies whose eyes were peeled on her. The women looked at each other and shrugged, continuing to mind their own business. She moved the merchandise around, busily performing the tasks that made up her shift, occasionally stopping to catch a breath. She'd pause and hold on to a nearby wall with one hand and her aching belly with the other. She'd feel her baby kick wildly inside her. But Selma clenched her teeth, closed her eyes, and just wished for the beckoning moves to disappear.

She left the store to examine the weather. Her shift was nearly over, her eyes were half-open and tired, and she was looking forward to going home. The rain had stopped a while ago and the streets had already dried in the sun, now looking clean and refreshed. The summer evening smelled of the boiled corn that was sold on the streets, wafting from barbeques at the neighboring houses. It made Selma hungry.

She watched the apartments in the building across the street as they turned livelier and brighter as people began to turn on lights. She wondered who lived in those houses, how they lived, whether they were filled with happiness or anxiety or agony, whether they had a job—lucrative or unprofitable. She wondered whether they had cousins or aunts in other corners of the globe sending them money, whether they had children they loved as if they were their only valuable possession in the world, whether they watched cartoons on a daily basis or glued their eyes to the video games on their phones. She wondered whether they ever came out to the store, perhaps to buy their favorite dessert, or if they skipped it sometimes because they could barely afford it. Had she ever seen them face to face? Had they ever spoken? As they usually did, her thoughts then turned back to the war. What had these people lived through? What kind of sacrifices had to be made, in blood or otherwise? Had they fought on the right side, had they wanted the war to happen so they could profiteer, had they overcome the worst of it? She contemplated all these scenarios, but suddenly the pain in her stomach disrupted her chain of thoughts. She bent down, hoping the position would ease the pain, but it only worsened it.

"What's happening to me," she whispered to herself.

She looked down between her legs and noticed her pants were wet. She touched them and brought her hand to her nose to smell the liquid. She couldn't discern what it could be. She wondered if she might have peed her pants so, out of embarrassment, she turned around and walked inside, heading straight to the bathroom.

The bathroom was tiny, consisting of a small sink in one corner and a toilet in the other.

She felt an incredible pain in her abdomen. She grabbed the sink and held it tight, waiting for the pain to go away. But the pain kept coming back, and it was getting worse and worse. Her contractions had begun.

She kneeled down and placed her forehead on the floor next to the toilet. She tried to manage the pain, clenching her teeth, grabbing her abdomen. She wanted to scream, but she was afraid she would be heard outside. She didn't want anyone to rush in and see her like this. She lay on the floor on her side, bent in half, knees as high as possible. Minutes had passed with the pain rotating in a whirlwind of wicked emotions. She felt her face wet; tears were falling down her face. The pain was unbearable.

Suddenly, she felt the pressure inside her. The baby was ready to come out. She recalled seeing a woman on her back one time in a movie, pushing to get her baby out, so she rolled over too, removed her clothes and began to push. She felt her pelvis opening up and the pain inside her throbbed down her legs.

Why is the baby not coming out? This was the only thought she could muster given her desire for the pain to end.

Before she could repeat the thought, she heard a baby's cry. A small creature lay on the floor, helpless and gasping for air. Selma craned her neck to view the new human. Its head was covered in black hair; its skin was red, eyes closed. She picked him up tentatively, almost afraid she would break him. Then she darted her eyes to the corner where she spotted a rag and, uncomfortably, turned around on her stomach to grab it with her free hand. She wrapped him up with the rag, hoping he'd retain the body heat that he was used to in her body. She took him in his arms and looked at him. By then, his cries had dwindled and he was making small movements. He didn't resemble anyone in particular, not his father or his mother. His face looked too small for any features to be pronounced yet.

Selma pulled the rag around him tightly. The baby seemed as if he was trying to open his eyes, but his lids were heavy and burdensome from being exposed to his new surroundings.

She was looking for a rope or similar to keep the rag tied around him, but the bathroom had nothing else. With difficulty, she stood up and placed him down on the floor for a few seconds while she fixed her clothes. Peering out through the gap in the door to ensure there was no one in her proximity, she then grabbed the baby and opened the bathroom door slowly.

She made a speedy exit, but instead of leaving by the front, she headed for the back door where a small opening to the street lay, isolated and lonely.

The dumpster was right out here, where the store disposed of empty boxes, cartons and damaged goods. She placed her son next to it then looked up at the sky, focusing on the Summer Triangle twinkling in all its glory. She heard her son cooing—he probably wanted to be fed, to be close to his mother, to retain the warmth of her belly. But all she did was bend down so she could fix the rag on his body one last time.

Then, she stood up, turned around, and walked away into the night.

❦ 10 ❦

BOSNIA AND HERZEGOVINA

EMMA FIDGETED IN HER PLANE SEAT, ANTICIPATING HER arrival in the Bosnian capital. She looked through the window and noticed the mountain tops peeking over the horizon. The scene looked like a postcard. She was exhausted from the red-eye flight, but the sense of renewed enthusiasm lifted her up as she kept thinking about why she was here, the new addition to her family.

A lot had happened in the last few years. No longer choosing to let herself be a victim, she resolved to pick up her things and move back to Chicago to be with her family, where the unconditional love and familiarity would nurture her soul.

While leaning her head against the plane window and listening to the engine roar with her eyes closed, Emma kept thinking about Michael and replayed the images of their last meaningful conversation. The interaction and images of Michael's face expressions were engrained in her brain as if she was recording a movie in slow motion and every move was amplified by its slowness.

"Are you sure?" Michael had said when she'd told him about moving to Chicago. He seemed to have been in denial. "Do you really think it's a good idea for us to be apart while I'm sorting things out?"

"This isn't about us, Michael. It appears that we want different things in life."

Michael nodded gently and gave her a nervous smile. He came up to her and hugged her, for the first time in a long time. Emma had forgotten what his hugs felt like, but this one made her feel uncomfortable. She didn't want it and so she tried to wiggle away from him. She didn't want his pity, or his empathy, or his sudden love.

"I'm leaving in a couple of weeks. I gave a notice at work."

"I don't know what to say. I'll miss you," Michael said, though he sounded as if he wasn't convinced of his own words. It simply might have been the shock. Though, Emma didn't feel anything. She wasn't moved by his words.

When she arrived in Chicago, she found herself a studio apartment a few blocks from her parents. Now that she was closer to them physically, her fear of losing her father to alcoholism suddenly diminished. As he aged, he had become wiser and less destructive. His drinking had dwindled over the years until he ditched it completely and took up rowing. While Emma dealt with life challenges of her own, her father was turning into a new, improved man. He'd wake up early in the morning—

around five a.m.—get ready and go to the nearby gym where he'd use the machines for a couple of hours. His strength was coming back, and thus, so was his confidence. Upon his retirement, he said he wanted to live a life that didn't consist of taking pills every day or visiting doctors on a frequent basis.

Her mother, Bella, was back to her old self, consumed by her job at a nearby school. As her retirement was also nearing, she'd secretly prayed to become a grandmother and to spend her aging years with Emma's child. Her hope had never diminished that it could happen.

Emma settled into her new studio apartment well. She placed a desk and a chair at one corner of a room, near the bay windows, from where she would conduct her new consulting business. Being her own boss was the best choice. She no longer cared about climbing up or falling off the corporate ladder, and would never have to worry about failing to meet someone's expectations. She woke up at her own leisure, met clients as she pleased, and went to bed when sleepy. Because this schedule afforded her more freedom, she felt content and confident. The old Emma had returned.

On the plane, Emma was sitting next to a young woman. This woman kept looking at her, and she could tell she was eager to start a conversation.

"Are you just visiting Sarajevo?" She asked once Emma had made eye contact.

"I am."

"Cool. I grew up in Sarajevo, but I live in Germany now. My parents and I moved there before the war."

"I'm so happy to hear that. I know the war was quite brutal."

Before her trip, Emma had tried to read up on the Bosnian War and the recent genocide. She wanted to familiarize herself with the history as much as possible. She couldn't quite fathom how all of that atrocity could transpire in the heart of Europe, allowing a whole nation to be wiped out in front of the eyes of so many influential people. She had seen glimpses of the war on TV, of course, but she'd never paid it much attention. For Emma, someone physically, mentally and emotionally removed from it all, the images on TV just looked like any rubble, like any tank, like any war. The victims were like any victims.

"My whole family and I lucked out," the woman continued. "We dodged that bullet. No pun attended." She laughed. "How long are you staying?"

"Just a few days." Emma was too tired to carry on a long and meaningful conversation and explain her intention of flying to Sarajevo.

"That's a short trip. But long enough to check out the city. Sarajevo is small."

As the plane descended, Emma could feel the pressure in her ears. The mountains came closer, and the peak of one came at her eye level. It seemed so mysterious in its depth and density. She wondered if the mountain could be visited. She had heard that a lot of the land was covered in mines and therefore it was dangerous to walk around in some places.

When the wheels hit the runway, and the plane

anchored on the ground, people began to clap. Emma turned around, confused at what the commotion was all about. The young woman sitting next to her noticed and she offered her an explanation, "It's what Bosnians do when they land safely."

"Is it common for planes to crash on the Sarajevo runway?"

"Oh no, not at all." The woman said. "It's just whenever there's even a smallest possibility of dying, they are happy to still be alive. Like during flying, you know."

They were escorted to the airport, a brisk walk on the runway. Emma tried to find the traces of the Tunnel of Hope, a tunnel she had learned was dug underneath the runway during the war, making it the only exit from the besieged city. But all she saw was a flat field with another mountain in the background.

There was a lot Emma wanted to learn about the Bosnian culture and the recent war. Nothing would make her happier than knowing where her child-to-be came from.

But wherever she tried, she felt overwhelmed by the complexity of the country's history.

Back home in Chicago, just as her life was turning around and she was beginning to feel human again, Emma heard from Catherine. She had called her one early morning, an odd time to just want to catch up. What she didn't know was that such an innocent gossip would end up changing her life.

"Hi sweetie, how are you?" she asked, sounding pleasant as always.

"I'm great." But Emma had no chance to reciprocate the question as Catherine continued on.

"Oh listen. I just heard...." The volume of her voice went down slightly. "I just heard that the Connors have adopted a baby."

The Connors were old mutual friends of theirs, high school sweethearts. Rumors went that Dan had reproductive issues and couldn't get Emily pregnant. It was supposed to be kept as a secret, but once the news leaked, it reached even the least curious ears. Emma didn't say anything in return.

"Did you know there was a huge Bosnian community in Chicago?" Catherine continued.

"Bosnian? No. Why would I know that?"

"Apparently, the Connors met a Bosnian couple who immigrated back in the early 90s. They ran away from the war and sought asylum in the US. I just found out there are thousands of Bosnians in the Chicago area."

"Okay." Emma was confused. She was too tired or still not awake enough to hear the seemingly significant news. "Why are you telling me all this?"

"The Bosnian couple gave the Connors the idea to adopt a baby in Bosnia. Apparently, a lot of children are left without parents because of the war. You mentioned once you'd looked into it, I thought it was a coincidence. I don't know. Think about it."

Ever since Amy, her therapist, planted the idea of adoption, Emma couldn't stop thinking about it. But with the move to Chicago and settling in her new abode, her mind dismissed it. Hearing from Catherine on this topic was the nudge to reconsider adoption. Out of curiosity, Emma opened up a web browser and looked it up. What a strange world. Nowadays, one could search for a human life with a click of a button. She felt like she was shopping.

The adoption happened like in a fairy tale. One day, she received an email from the adoption agency in Bosnia matching her up with a three-year old boy. At first, she thought it was as scam, a dirty joke someone was playing her. But when she read further and saw the photograph of a beautiful boy, the experience became too real. The date to pick up and unite with the child was spelled out: September 12, 2012.

She waited for months to unite with her son, and the day was finally here, and it was mostly sunny with the rays penetrating through small white clouds. The air felt clean and welcoming; the temperature was just about perfect. In her hotel room, Emma put on her best suit and carefully put her make up on. While she combed her hair in the mirror, she noticed a slight apprehension in her demeanor, nervousness about the union with her new child.

I hope it goes well. Her dream of becoming a mother was getting closer with every minute. All she wanted was for the child to embrace her and feel her warmth.

Outside the hotel, she hailed a taxi. The driver waved her in, realizing she was a foreigner immediately.

"Where to?" he asked in English.

"Mojmilo, please."

During the ride, the driver wanted to talk to her, be

hospitable and entertaining, but Emma was too nervous to concentrate. All she had on her mind was the small child she was about to meet and more importantly bring into her family. The taxi driver's words flew right by her and she had no room for reciprocation or small talk.

The orphanage consisted of several houses lined up in a row on a lonesome hill across from high-rise buildings. Even from a distance, Emma could see buildings across from the orphanage covered in the multitude of bullet holes. The Mojmilo hill, Emma learned, had been occupied by the Serb paramilitary groups at the beginning of the war from which they were shooting mortars onto the streets. Emma felt tears spring from her eyes.

When the taxi driver turned around to inform her they had arrived, Emma reached for her face to wipe the tears.

"Everything okay?" The driver asked robotically.

"Yes, everything is fine. How much?"

When he told her the amount, she reached out for a single bill and handed it to him. "Keep the change." She had no patience to wait. Only when she stood on the street near the orphanage did she feel the reality setting in. She consciously placed her right hand on her left one so to stop it from shaking. The sky was turning gray, and she rushed to the orphanage gate to flee from the fast-changing colors.

A young man came out of one of the houses and cheerfully greeted her, "Hi, welcome. You must be Emma."

"Yes, yes." She was relieved to have met the person in

charge of the adoption. It wasn't a hoax or a dream after all. She really was adopting a child in Bosnia.

"Come on in." He ushered her into a house that smelled of freshly baked bread and stew. They passed by what looked like a kitchen, where a couple of women were busily walking back and forth, and entered a small office where the man gestured for her to sit down and said to make herself comfortable.

"Would you like anything? Coffee? Water?"

"Oh, no, thanks." There was a knot in her stomach and she didn't feel she could handle a drink.

"How was your flight here?"

"Quite uneventful. But I am jet lagged. A seven-hour difference is no small feat for me."

The man let out a gentle laugh. "The things we do for our children."

"True." Emma offered a smile, relishing the way he said 'our children.' Further confirmation that her little boy was actually hers. "I wouldn't mind traveling to the end of the world."

She was trying not to show how nervous she was in case it proved to be detrimental to their opinions on her suitability for motherhood.

"We're always happy for our children when they find a safe and loving home. That is our mission here. We know that Nusret will be in good hands after he leaves here."

"I'm glad you entrusted me with such a beautiful child. I can't wait to meet him."

"He's ready for you." The man's words vibrated through her ears. *He's ready*. She needed to hear those words to break up her nerves. She promised herself she'd be the best mother she could be. She'd love this child unconditionally as if he had come out of her womb. It didn't make a difference that he was brought into the world by people unknown to her who most likely had a legitimate reason to give up their son for adoption.

"If I may ask, what happened to his parents, do you know?"

"His father is unfit to be a single parent, and his mother.... She seems to have disappeared. We heard from the grapevine that she moved to another country—no one knows which one exactly. Someone found her in her apartment a few days before she disappeared. She'd attempted suicide—took too many pills—but they took her to the hospital and pumped out her stomach."

"Why did she attempt suicide?" As soon as she said those words, Emma regretted it. She felt naïve and ignorant.

"That'd be like asking why the sky is blue on a perfectly sunny day."

Emma wasn't quite sure what the man meant by that; the problem could be in translation, but she didn't ask for clarification, especially as his next words filled her heart with such joy.

"I believe your son is ready to meet you now."

He stood up and signaled for her to follow him. They walked down the hallway in what appeared to be a maze. She felt dizzy from the accrued tension in her heart. She was too nervous to be excited. But with each step, her face formed a bigger and bigger smile until they arrived in the room where her son was waiting for her.

When they stepped inside, Nusret was slouched in a small chair, looking down at the floor. He looked like a miniature man dressed in a white shirt and a black suit, his hair combed to one side. When he heard the steps getting closer, he looked up to rest his eyes on his new mother. He'd never met his biological mother and he knew he would never find out if he ever meant anything to her. His eyes, which were a deep brown, looked sad yet inquisitive. His new home, which was still so far away, beckoned a promise for a better life.

When he saw Emma, he cracked a smile, with his cheek dimple dancing on his left cheek. He started to say something in Bosnian, and even though Emma couldn't understand a word, she just smiled. Still shocked from this actually being real, she stood there unable to move, admiring the beautiful little creature that would soon occupy her home and her heart.

"What did he say?" She turned to the man and asked.

"He's saying that he made his bed and put away his toys."

Now that seeing the boy set a new note, Emma woke up from what felt like a beautiful dream only to find it was real. She walked up to the little boy.

"*Zdravo*," she said. She'd learned the greeting in a Bosnia travel guide.

The boy looked at her and smiled coyly, knowing that her Bosnian was limited. She extended her arms, inviting the boy to come to her embrace. He slowly stood up and approached her, before throwing himself into her arms. She squeezed him gently, for he felt fragile and small. She sniffed his hair; he smelled of baby shampoo. Dumbfounded by the physical touch of her child, she began to cry, and carefully tried to conceal the shaking.

Ever so gently, the boy came closer and, in English, whispered in her ear, "I love you."

The man explained that was the only phrase in English the boy knew. That was all she needed to hear.

For Emma, it was a most glorious day. It was the day her life started anew.

THANK YOU!

I sincerely thank you for reading this book!

As an indie author, you can support me by leaving a review, even if it's only a sentence, checking out my other books, and subscribing to my website. I'm also happy to answer any questions you may have, so do please get in touch with me via my website:

https://nadijamujagic.com

LET'S KEEP IN TOUCH!

I love to hear from my readers and also share news on my new releases, free content and book promos! For updates, please make sure to subscribe on: https://nadijamujagic.com

ACKNOWLEDGMENTS

I'd like to thank Christine Vecitis for being my first and alpha reader of the novel, and giving me important critical feedback for the book. Next, I'd like to thank my husband, Chad, for reading and offering suggestions for making my book sound ever better. I thank Rady Rogers, my friend, who beta read the novel and for her honest response to the main characters. Finally, my two editors, Emily and Julie, true professionals whose assistance helped put the book in better shape. Thank you for believing in me! Your support is needed and appreciated — it means a world.